**The woman's lips tilted up at the corners briefly as she drove out onto the street. "Hank has resources most people don't. Not even the government."**

Rip riffled through the contents of the packet, glancing at a passport with his picture on it, a name he wasn't familiar with on the document. "Chuck Gideon?"

"Better get used to it."

"Speaking of names...we've already kissed and you haven't told me who you are." Rip glanced her way briefly.

Her eyes narrowed and her lips firmed. "No, I haven't."

"Is it a secret, or are you going to tell me?"

"It's probably best if I don't tell you my real name."

"Why? Do you have a shady past, or are you related to someone important?"

"For this mission, I'm related to someone important." She twisted her lips and sent a crooked grin his way. "You. For the purpose of this operation, you can call me Phyllis. Phyllis Gideon. I'll be your wife."

# NAVY SEAL NEWLYWED

---

**New York Times** Bestselling Author
## ELLE JAMES

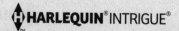

This book is dedicated to all the families of military personnel
who have kept the home fires burning and welcomed
their loved ones home with open arms.

ISBN-13: 978-0-373-69837-0

Recycling programs
for this product may
not exist in your area.

Navy SEAL Newlywed

Copyright © 2015 by Mary Jernigan

Printed in U.S.A.

**Elle James**, a *New York Times* bestselling author, started writing when her sister challenged her to write a romance novel. She has managed a full-time job and raised three wonderful children, and she and her husband even tried ranching exotic birds (ostriches, emus and rheas). Ask her, and she'll tell you what it's like to go toe-to-toe with an angry 350-pound bird! Elle loves to hear from fans at ellejames@earthlink.net or ellejames.com.

## Books by Elle James

### HARLEQUIN INTRIGUE

#### Covert Cowboys, Inc. series

*Triggered*
*Taking Aim*
*Bodyguard Under Fire*
*Cowboy Resurrected*
*Navy SEAL Justice*
*Navy SEAL Newlywed*

#### Thunder Horse series

*Hostage to Thunder Horse*
*Thunder Horse Heritage*
*Thunder Horse Redemption*
*Christmas at Thunder Horse Ranch*

Visit the Author Profile page at Harlequin.com for more titles.

# CAST OF CHARACTERS

**"Rip" Cord Schafer**—Navy SEAL undercover as a billionaire playboy to discover the traitor selling arms to terrorists in Honduras.

**Tracie Kosart**—Former FBI special agent and the first female "cowboy" to work for Hank Derringer's Covert Cowboys, Inc. First assignment is to go undercover as a bride to an equally fake billionaire playboy.

**Hank Derringer**—Billionaire willing to take the fight for justice into his own hands by setting up CCI—Covert Cowboys, Inc.

**Dan Greer**—DEA agent undercover in Honduras in a terrorist training camp, killed during his extraction.

**Carmelo Del Gado**—Honduran coffee plantation owner with possible link to a Honduran terrorist training camp.

**Vance Tate**—Salesman at Blackburn Gun Manufacturing.

**Mark Kuntz**—Senator Thomas Craine's executive assistant, former Special Forces soldier.

**Senator Thomas Craine**—Senator involved in negotiating trade agreements with Central American countries.

**Hector Devita**—Businessman with a successful security firm providing bodyguards and security systems to the wealthy Hondurans.

**Carlos Sanchez, Julio Jiminez and Zach Adams**—Former SEALs working for Hank with the Covert Cowboys, Inc.

**Ben Harding**—Former cop in the Austin Police Department, fired because he killed a man with his bare hands. Now working for Hank with the Covert Cowboys, Inc.

**Chuck Bolton**—Wounded soldier returning to Wild Oak Canyon to join Hank Derringer's team, Covert Cowboys, Inc.

**Thorn Drennan**—Former small-town sheriff now working for Hank with the Covert Cowboys, Inc.

# Chapter One

Hunkered low in the underbrush, Navy SEAL Chief Petty Officer "Rip" Cord Schafer gripped the M4A1 rifle with the SOPMOD upgrade and inched forward, carefully placing every step to avoid tripping, snapping branches or making any other loud noises. Loaded with sixty pounds of equipment specially selected for this mission, he was ready for anything.

Gunny took point, leading the team into the Honduran camp, keeping to the darkness of the jungle. Moonlight shimmered through the occasional break in the dense overhead canopy, barely making it down to the jungle floor.

Rip had his headset in one ear and listened for sounds of the camp with his other.

Montana eased up behind Gunny, followed by Sawyer, then the newest SEAL, Gosling, with Rip bringing up the rear.

Their mission: extract one undercover DEA agent from a terrorist training camp deep in the jungle of Honduras.

No matter where he looked, Rip could detect no sentries standing guard or patrolling the compound. Strange. The DEA agent had been adamant about being pulled out. He'd feared for his life and had been concerned the information he needed to pass on might be lost.

In his brief plea to be extracted, he'd given specific

*GPS coordinates. When Gunny reached the position, he held up his fist.*

*The team stopped in place and hugged the earth, waiting.*

*He pointed to Montana and Sawyer and gave them the follow-me sign.*

*The three surrounded the door of the building. Gunny nudged it open and disappeared inside. Montana and Sawyer followed. Gosling and Rip remained outside, providing cover.*

*Seconds later, they hustled out a man wearing rumpled clothing, his shoulder-length hair straggly and unkempt. He ducked low and moved quickly between them, hurrying toward the path leading out of the camp.*

*Gunny motioned for Gosling and Rip to fall in with the team. They had their man, and it appeared as though they were going to make a clean getaway with none of the terrorists aware of the agent's departure.*

*The hair on the back of Rip's neck stood straight up. The entire mission had been too easy. If there was any real danger, wouldn't there have been sentries on alert, wielding machine guns and willing to cut down anyone who stepped into range?*

*They cleared the edge of the camp, heading back to the river and the waiting boat.*

*Gunny was in the lead again, followed by Sawyer. Montana was in front of their extracted DEA agent and Gosling behind him.*

*The agent stumbled for a moment.*

*Gosling didn't adjust his stride in time. He caught up with the man then gave him a hand to right himself.*

*The sharp report of gunfire ripped through the night, shattering the silence.*

*Gosling collapsed where he stood.*

*Another shot rang out and the DEA agent grunted and crumpled to the ground.*

*Instinct made the remaining members of the SEAL team drop to their bellies.*

*His heart slamming into his ribs, adrenaline racing through his veins, Rip low crawled to the two men who'd been hit. He shone his red penlight over Gosling. The man had taken the bullet in the throat. By the dark stain spreading in a wide blob on the ground around him, Rip suspected the bullet had cut a hole in the young SEAL's jugular vein. He lay sprawled on his side, his body completely still. Rip covered the wound with his hand, but nothing he did could slow the flow of blood.*

*"Roll call," Gunny spoke into Rip's headset. One by one the other team members reported in.*

*"Montana."*

*"Sawyer."*

*"Schafer," Rip said. His heart in his throat, he reported, "Gosling took a hit."*

*Sawyer spun around and low crawled with his weapon in front of him to where Gosling lay unmoving. He jerked Rip's hand off the wound. "Damn."*

*Gunny muttered a curse, "Status."*

*For a moment Rip closed his eyes, thinking of his last conversation with the young petty officer. Gosling's wife was expecting their first child. He'd been so proud, scared and excited all at once.*

*Sawyer answered, "Gosling's dead."*

*Though Rip knew it, hearing Sawyer's confirmation made it all the more real and heartbreaking. Overwhelmed with grief but knowing they still had to get the agent out, he moved toward the other downed man a yard away. The agent had been hit in the chest. Without the armor plate the SEALs wore in their vests, he hadn't been protected.*

"Our guest?" Gunny demanded.

Rip felt for a pulse. As he pressed his fingers to the base of the man's throat, a hand snaked out and grabbed his wrist with surprising strength.

In the darkness of the night, Rip could see the whites of the man's eyes staring up at him.

"Set up," the agent said, his voice nothing more than a guttural whisper. He reached up to the medallion around his neck, yanked it free and pressed it into Rip's hand. "Find out who."

"Who what?" Rip asked.

"Status on our extraction?" Gunny's voice sounded loud in Rip's ear.

"Conscious, but not good," Rip replied, stuffing the medallion into his pocket.

Shouts could be heard in the village behind them as the occupants raised the alarm. Lights blinked on and headlights lit the night. The tap, tap, tap of gunfire broke through the night's silence.

"Let's get out of here." Gunny raced back to where Sawyer and Rip were leaning over the wounded men. "I'll take the agent."

The agent gripped Rip's arm and refused to let go.

Rip straightened, bringing the man up and throwing him over his shoulder. "I've got the agent. Get Gosling. He deserves a proper burial."

Cursing, Gunny hesitated only a moment before pitching Gosling over his shoulder, muttering, "This wasn't the way this was supposed to go down, damn it."

Rip didn't wait. With the deadweight of the wounded agent bearing down on him, he took off at an awkward lope racing through the trees and vines toward the boat they'd left in the nearby river. Silence wasn't necessary. Speed was.

*Montana ran ahead to get the boat engines started. Sawyer brought up the rear, covering their sixes as Rip and Gunny carried their burdens over the uneven floor of the jungle.*

*Shots rang out behind them. A vehicle full of angry terrorists raced toward them. Sawyer held them at bay, firing short bursts of rounds into the night. He ejected his clip and without missing a beat slammed another home while running backward to keep up with the other SEALs.*

*When Rip reached the boat, he jumped on board and laid his charge on the deck. He manned his position behind a grenade launcher, waiting for Sawyer to emerge from the tree line.*

*Gunny jumped on board, dropped Gosling on deck and took a position behind a machine gun.*

*As soon as Sawyer cleared the trees, Gunny opened fire on the oncoming sets of headlights.*

*Rip launched a grenade, aiming at the line of vehicles barreling through the underbrush.*

*As Sawyer leaped aboard, Montana hit the throttle, spun the craft around on the water and gunned it, sending it speeding downriver, bullets plinking off the hull and hitting the water around them.*

*Not until they were a good mile downstream did Rip glance down at Sawyer working over the body of the DEA agent.*

*Rip shook his head. The mission had gone like clockwork. They'd been out of the village, on their way back. What the hell had happened? Rip glanced at his teammate's lifeless body on the deck of the boat. Gosling was dead. Two shots were fired and then none until the terrorists had loaded up in their trucks and given chase.*

*Whoever had fired the first two shots could have taken out more, if not all, of the SEAL team. Why hadn't he?*

*When the boat reached the helicopter landing zone, Sawyer rocked back on his heels, his shoulders slumped.*

*Gunny shot a glance back at him. "Well?"*

*Sawyer shook his head. "He's dead."*

"HEY, SWEETIE, WOULD you like a drink?"

Rip blinked up at the waitress standing beside him with a tray in her hands. For a full thirty seconds he couldn't remember where he was. He'd done it again. The shrinks he'd seen in the past had said part of post-traumatic stress disorder was flashbacks to events that had an indelible impact on him.

"Excuse me?" he said, buying time for his mind to reconnect with his surroundings.

"Would you like a drink?" the waitress repeated.

He shook his head. "No, thank you."

The woman moved away to the next customer in the casino.

Rip stared around at row after row of brightly lit slot machines, pinging, ringing or plinking in the darkness. For a long moment he wondered how the hell he'd gone from a hot, humid, bug- and snake-infested jungle to an upscale casino in Mississippi.

Then he remembered all the events that had led up to this meeting. All that had happened since getting back from Honduras.

He stared around the dimly lit room.

*What's keeping him?*

The past six weeks since their failed mission had been a blur. Rip had been back on duty with his team, while covertly researching the odd medallion the DEA agent had shoved into his hand.

The medallion had been a clever disguise for an electronic storage device on which were stored hundreds of photos of the terrorist training camp and crates of American-made weapons and ammunition disguised as World Health Organization donations.

And based on the botched mission in Honduras, someone higher up didn't want the agent or anyone else exposing who was providing the weapons from the States. How else could a sniper have known exactly when and where they would be unless someone had tipped them off?

Rip had pilfered a copy of the after-action report, developed the pictures and was in the process of piecing things together when an assassin started stalking him. He'd found out that details of their mission had been leaked. Not only after its failure, but before it had even been launched.

Someone, possibly in a high-ranking political position, wanted that agent dead and had sent the SEALs in to get him out of the village and into the open so a sniper could take him out. It was the only answer he could come up with given the limited information he had.

Rip was in hiding, officially missing and presumed dead. The Navy still thought he'd been swallowed by the Pearl River after being shot during a live-fire training mission with Navy SEALs Special Boat Team 22. If not for the help of former SEAL James "Cowboy" Monahan and Rip's old friend FBI Agent Melissa Bradley, Rip might not still be alive. The two had persevered, and searched the river until they found him holed up in a shack in the Mississippi bayou.

*Lucky me.* Rip snorted.

Now, after spending the past three weeks recovering from his gunshot wound, Rip was finally able to pursue his self-appointed mission.

He'd gotten his commander and the few members of his team who'd been involved in his rescue to keep his survival on the down low until he could find the persons responsible for the death of the undercover DEA agent.

He couldn't engage his team in this mission without disclosing to the world and to whoever was responsible for the assassination of the agent that the Navy's Chief Petty Officer Cord Schafer was alive and well. In order to keep from becoming a target again, it was best if he remained "dead" until he resolved the situation.

Only, he knew he couldn't do it on his own. He needed a partner, a cover and fake passports to get him down to Honduras without raising red flags to the terrorist organization or the traitorous Americans supplying them with weapons.

Sitting in a crowded casino in Biloxi, Mississippi, with a baseball cap pulled low over his brow, he waited for his contact, not knowing who he was or what he looked like, only that Cowboy's new boss, billionaire Hank Derringer, was sending one of his operatives from Covert Cowboys, Inc.

Rip glanced up every time a man slowed near the slot machine he was only halfheartedly playing. He looked for a man in a cowboy hat and boots, but most of the men in the place were hatless, gray-haired and wearing comfortable loafers.

Glancing at his watch once again, he started getting nervous. He hadn't been out in public since the mercenary had shot him. Feeling exposed, he sat at the designated position in the selected casino, at the exact time he was supposed to meet his contact.

Where the hell was his cowboy?

Shoving another token into the machine, he punched the spin button without caring what pictures he'd land on. He was surprised when three cherries lined up on the screen and tokens plinked into the tray below.

Soft, slender hands slid over his shoulders and down the

front of his chest, and a sultry voice whispered in his ear, "Getting lucky, sweetheart?"

Nerves stretched to the breaking point, Rip fought the urge to grab the arm, spin around and slam the person to the floor. Instead, he spun on the stool in such a way he had the woman sitting across his lap before she knew his intentions.

Her eyes widened briefly and then narrowed. "Wanna take your winnings and buy me a drink?" She had long dark brown hair, green eyes and a lean, athletic figure dressed in a red cotton sundress that screamed tourist.

Though he gave the appearance of being happy to see her, his hand on her wrist was tight. She wouldn't get away easily or without raising a ruckus. He smiled at her and, through his teeth, he demanded, "Who the hell are you?"

She smiled back at him, cupped his face with her other hand and patted his cheek, not so gently. "I'm your contact, so play nice and pretend you're happy to see me."

For a brief moment he frowned.

She laughed out loud. "If that's happy, you're a terrible actor. Make like we're a couple."

"Since I didn't get the memo, I'm a little slow on the uptake. Let me set the stage." Getting past the shock of his contact's gender, Rip had to admit she was a lot prettier than any cowboy he might have expected. He wrapped his arm around her waist, then slid his hand up into her dark brown hair and pressed the back of her neck, angling her face toward his.

"What are you doing?" she said, her eyes widening.

"I would think it was obvious. I'm showing you how happy I am to see you." Then he captured her mouth in a deep, lip-crushing kiss.

Apparently she was so shocked that her mouth opened. Rip slid his tongue in and caressed the length of hers.

At first her hands, trapped between them, pressed against his chest. But after a moment or two, her fingers curled into his shirt and she kissed him back.

When he finally came up for air, it took him a second or two to come back to his senses and remember where he was, yet again.

He stood so quickly, he had to steady her on her feet before he let go of her. "Let's get out of here."

"What about your winnings?" she said.

He scooped up enough tokens for two full cups, carried them over to a gray-haired senior citizen and dumped them into her slot machine tray. "Congratulations, you're a winner." He kissed the woman's cheek, grabbed his contact's hand and headed for the door.

The woman whose hand he held hurried to keep up with him in her bright red cowboy boots. "You were playing the dollar slots."

"So?" he countered.

"That was probably a couple hundred dollars."

"Then that woman will go home happy."

He tipped his baseball cap lower over his forehead, slid his arm around her waist and smiled down at her as he stepped out into the sauna-like Mississippi late afternoon sunshine. "Where's your car?"

"This way." She guided him to the parking lot and stopped beside a large black 4x4 truck with twenty-inch rims and tinted windows.

"Seriously?" Rip shook his head. "This is yours?"

"One of the perks of working for Hank Derringer. That and an arsenal of every weapon you could possibly need." When she hit the key fob, the engine started and the doors unlocked. She opened the driver's side door and nodded to the passenger seat. "Hop in."

"How do I know you really work for Hank?"

"You don't. But has anyone else shown up and told you he's your contact?"

"No."

"You have that." She raised her eyebrows, the saucy expression doing funny things to his insides. "So, do you trust me, or not?"

His lips curled upward on the ends. "I'll go with not."

"Oh, come on, sweetheart." She batted her pretty green eyes and gave him a sexy smile. "What's not to trust?"

His gaze scraped over her form. "I expected a cowboy, not a…"

"Cow*girl*?" Her smile sank and she slipped into the driver's seat. "I grew up on a ranch, I've worked with cattle and horses and I know the value of a hard day's work. I spent eight years with the FBI. I also know right from wrong and tend to be loyal to a fault, until the person or organization I believe in breaks my trust." Her lips firmed into a straight line. "Are you coming or not? If you're dead set on a cowboy, I'll contact Hank and tell him to send a male replacement. But then he'd have to come up with another plan."

Rip considered her words and then acknowledged he didn't have a lot of choices with only a couple of week's reprieve before he had to turn up alive or be buried by the government. He rounded the front of the truck and climbed into the passenger seat. "I'll go along for the ride and maybe you can convince me you're up for the challenge."

"Please. I don't normally have to justify my existence to the people I work with. I'm a trained operative. I don't need this assignment. However, from what Hank told me, you need all the help you can get."

"I'm interested in how you and Hank plan to provide that help. Frankly, I'd rather my SEAL team had my six."

"Yeah, but you're deceased. Using your SEAL team would only alert your assassin that you aren't as dead as the Navy claims you are. How long do you think you'll last once that bit of news leaks out?"

His lips pressed together. "I'd survive."

"By going undercover? Then you still won't have the backing of your team, and we're back to the original plan." She grinned. "Me."

Rip sighed. "Fine. I want to head back to Honduras and trace the weapons back to where they're coming from. What's Hank's plan?"

"For me to work with you." She pulled a large envelope from between her seat and the console and handed it across to him. "Everything we need is in that packet. Passports, cash, credit cards and new identities. We also have at our disposal Hank's jet, a Citation X, capable of cruising at Mach 0.9, almost the speed of sound. Say the word and we can be in the sky within twenty minutes. It's waiting at the airport."

Monahan had only good things to say about Hank and all he could do for the operation, otherwise Rip would have been more hesitant getting the billionaire involved. With a DEA agent and one of his SEAL teammates dead, and himself almost killed, he was determined to find the one responsible. But after losing one of his SEAL brothers, he was hesitant about getting anyone else caught in the crosshairs. "Hank sure pulled all of this together fast."

The woman's lips tilted up briefly as she drove out onto the street. "Hank has resources most people don't. Not even the government."

Rip riffled through the contents of the packet, glancing at a passport with his picture on it as well as a name he'd never seen. "Chuck Gideon?"

"Better get used to it."

"Speaking of names…we've already kissed and you haven't told me who you are." Rip glanced her way briefly.

Her eyes narrowed and her lips firmed. "No, I haven't."

"Is it a secret? Do you have a shady past or are you re-lated to someone important."

"For this mission, I'm related to someone important." She twisted her lips and sent a crooked grin his way. "You. For the purpose of this operation, you can call me Phyllis. Phyllis Gideon. I'll be your wife."

## Chapter Two

Tracie Kosart had recognized the man in the casino immediately from the photo Hank Derringer had given her and realized that could be a problem. Even with his shaggy long hair, the breadth of his shoulders, the stubborn set of his chin and the steely look in his gray-blue eyes set him apart from the other gamblers there hoping to score a big win.

Though he'd been slouching on the stool, he looked as if he could spring into action at a moment's notice. Now as he sat opposite her in the interior of her truck, he filled the space, his shoulders seeming to block her entire view.

"Phyllis, huh?" He stared at her, his eyes narrowing. "You don't look like a Phyllis."

"It doesn't matter." When he looked at her so intently, it made her body heat and her belly tighten.

"Missy?"

"What?"

"Jasmine, Lois, Penelope? I could list names all day." He pinned her with his stare, a sassy smirk on his face. "You might as well tell me."

"Penelope?" She shot a glance at him, her mouth twitching as she fought a smile. "You think I look like a Penelope?"

"Some parents have a sense of humor." He raised his brows. "Well?"

She sighed. "Tracie. My name's Tracie Kosart."

"That's better." He stuck out his hand. "Nice to meet you, Tracie. And by the way, the name fits you better than Phyllis."

She took one hand off the steering wheel to shake his, an electrical surge racing up her arm from their joined fingers. Tracie yanked her hand back and wrapped it tightly around the steering wheel, willing the surge of fiery heat to fade.

"You and Derringer seem to have this all worked out." Rip leaned back in his set. "Where to first?"

"We've looked over all the photos the dead agent left you, along with the after-action report from the extraction operation and we really don't have much to go on. Yes, they prove the terrorists are receiving American-made weapons in World Health Organization boxes. But we don't know for certain who is sending them or at what point they are packaged to ship via WHO." Tracie shifted the big truck into Drive and pulled out of the parking lot.

Rip nodded. "I'm betting the World Health Organization didn't send those boxes."

"What we need is one of those guns so that we can trace the serial number on it back to the manufacturer. Short of going to Honduras to get one, we should exhaust all other stateside options first."

"Okay, what options?" The SEAL beside her crossed his arms, which made his biceps appear bigger than they already did.

Tracie had to focus on the road to keep from openly drooling. The man had testosterone oozing from every pore. For a moment she forgot Rip's question—then it came back to her. "I was hoping you had some ideas. We think the DEA agent's boss had to have been receiving data from him. He might have other operatives inside the terrorist group or in nearby towns."

"And how do we find Dan Greer's boss?"

Tracie snorted softly. "Hank already has. He was able to tap into the DEA database and extract that information." Hank had the connections, the computer power and a technical guru who could tap into any system.

"I'm surprised Hank hasn't already contacted the agent's boss."

A muffled beep sounded in the console between them. Tracie lifted a cell phone out of a cup holder and glanced down at a text. Her lips formed a broad smile. "As a matter of fact, he has. We have a meeting with Morris Franks in Atlanta in three hours."

Rip gave her a doubtful smile. "Honey, it takes a lot longer than three hours to drive to Atlanta."

She turned onto a highway and jerked her head toward a green sign with an airplane depicted in white. "What did I say about having Hank's Citation X available?" Tracie softened. As a former FBI agent, she remembered how unbelievable Hank's assets were when she'd first been exposed to them. "Prepare to be impressed."

Instead of driving through the terminal area of the Biloxi airport, she drove on to the private businesses' hangars along the runway and parked outside one of them.

As they climbed out of the truck, the door to the structure opened and a man stepped out. "Right this way, Mr. & Mrs. Gideon. I'm Tom Callahan. We've topped off the fuel, your pilot has performed the preflight checklist and he's filed the flight plan. The jet is ready for takeoff whenever you two say the word." Tom smiled. "And congratulations on your recent marriage."

Tracie almost did a double take until she remembered that was their cover story. "Th-thank you."

A hand settled at the small of her back. "It all happened

so quickly, we're still getting used to it, aren't we, dear?"
Rip guided her through the doorway into a reception area.

Tom led the way past a desk to another door that opened
into the hangar where a shiny new Citation X airplane sat
on the tarmac. The huge hangar door slid open, sunlight
cutting a wide swath into the dim interior.

"Shall we?" Tracie asked.

Rip waved a hand. "Ladies first." Tracie climbed the
short set of stairs into the cabin and took the first seat on
the far side.

Ducking to keep from bumping his head, Rip entered
the cabin and dropped into the seat beside her.

As soon as they were aboard, a flight attendant pulled
the door closed, and the engines ignited.

Soon the small jet, with seating for twelve, taxied down
the runway and lifted smoothly into the air.

"Okay, now I'm impressed," Rip whispered. "How long
will it take to get to Atlanta?"

Tracie glanced at her watch. "We should be there in less
than an hour. In the meantime, we should go over what
data the DEA agent was able to pass off before he died and
the after-action report, one more time to see if we missed
anything."

RIP STARED ACROSS the narrow aisle at Tracie.

With her long, slender legs crossed at the knees and one
of her red high heels bouncing with barely leashed energy,
she still didn't look like a trained operative. He was less
than thrilled at the idea of Hank sending a woman to help
him. He'd rather have had a man to work with. Women
tended to complicate things. His natural urge to protect
women and children might get in the way of a successful operation. *This operation has been dangerous thus far*

*and will only get worse. I'm not entirely sold on the idea of working with a woman.*

"If it makes you feel any better, I used to work for the FBI. I received my training at Quantico and I've been a field agent for more than five years. I worked undercover along the Mexican border to help stop several drug- and human-trafficking rings. I know how to handle a gun, and I'm not afraid to use one."

Rip nodded in deference to her risky and dangerous duty assignments. "Have you ever been in the jungles of Honduras?"

"No, but I've been held hostage in a cave in Mexico and survived. I know what hard work, prior planning and enemy engagement is all about. Don't let the dress fool you." She raised her hand, holding the cell phone up. "But, if you're still worried about working with a woman, I can contact Hank now and have him send another agent to replace me."

He liked her spunk and the fact she wasn't taking any crap from him. Rip sat back in his seat. "What I don't understand is why Hank sent you. I thought he was all about cowboys."

She shrugged, making that movement look entirely too sexy, her creamy white shoulders in stark contrast with the bright red dress. "As I already mentioned. I grew up on a ranch. Hank likes his cowboys—or girls—to have that ranch-life work ethic and sense of morals and values."

"I don't know Hank Derringer. All I have to go on is my buddy Jim Monahan's word."

Tracie's lips quirked upward and she stared out the window. "Hank and his team saved my life. I have nothing but respect for the work they do."

"Just what is it he does?" Rip asked.

"He champions the truth and justice when other organizations can't seem to get it right or have corruption in their ranks." As she spoke, her jaw hardened and her mouth pulled into a tight line.

"Why did you give up on the FBI?" Rip asked.

"You know that part about corruption in the ranks?" She snorted. "Well, let's just say, I wouldn't be alive if I had relied only on the organization I had sworn into."

"Surely not all of the FBI is rotten." Rip studied her.

Tracie glanced his way. "No, not all of the agents are. But Hank made me an offer I couldn't refuse. After two of the agents I worked with went bad, I was ready for a fresh start."

Rip turned away and stared out the window. He knew how she felt. As a member of the Navy SEALs, Rip had been trained to rely on his brothers in arms. When one went bad, as one had on the mission in Honduras, it shook his entire foundation of trust. Especially since the bad apple had been the leader of the mission, the now deceased Gunnery Sergeant Frank Petit. Rip's friend, James Monahan, a man he'd put his complete faith in, had helped to expose Gunny for the traitor he was.

What worried him even more was that they still had no idea who had paid Gunny to leak the information about their mission. He suspected it was someone higher up. Someone in Washington.

For a long moment, he sat in silence, reliving the past few weeks. He was only just recovered from the assassin's gunshot wound. If not for his best friend and a former SEAL teammate, he wouldn't have made it. That fact alone gave him hope for humanity. There were good people out there. His glance shifted to Tracie. She might be one of them. Only time would tell.

After what seemed like only a handful of minutes, the jet began its descent into Atlanta.

The plane's tires kissed the runway with barely a bounce

and, after rolling it into an open hangar, the pilot brought the aircraft to a complete stop.

The flight attendant lowered the stairs and stood to the side.

Rip stepped down first into the dim interior of the hangar and held out his hand to Tracie.

For a moment, she refused his proffered hand, her brow puckering. Then she laid her fingers in his.

The last time he and Tracie touched, he'd felt an electric jolt. This time was no different and the fire raced all the way through Rip's body. What was it about the woman that had his body on high sexual alert? To get his mind off her, he leaned close and asked, "If the DEA agent was terminated for what he knew, how has his boss managed to stay alive?"

Tracie nodded. "Perhaps he doesn't know anything."

Rip ground to a halt. "In that case, we're wasting our time."

"We won't know that until we meet with him." Without slowing, Tracie strode across the hangar lengthening the distance between them.

A man appeared at a doorway. "This way Mr. and Mrs. Gideon. Your car is waiting."

Rather than be left in the hangar, Rip ran to catch up, falling in step beside Tracie.

A sleek black limousine waited at the curb, the chauffeur holding the door. He didn't speak a word as he held the door open while Tracie and Rip slid inside.

Once the door was closed, Tracie turned to Rip. "Have you considered the fact that Morris Franks's willingness to talk to us might be an indication he knew more than he let on to others in his own department?"

Rip's eyes narrowed and he stared out the windshield

as if trying to see into the future. "Or, he could be looking for more information himself."

"I suppose we'll know soon enough. The hotel isn't far from the airport."

Tracie sat across the limo from Rip, not any single part of her body or limbs so much as touching him. Rip found himself wanting to reach across the short distance and pull her into his arms. The scent of her hair was doing strange things to him. Funny that even with her incredible legs and the classy way the red dress fit her body, the smell of her shampoo was what got to him most. It set every one of his nerves on edge and his groin tightened.

As a SEAL assigned to Special Boat Team 22—conducting missions and training their own team for missions as well as other SEAL teams—he hadn't had the time nor the inclination to pursue a lasting romantic relationship. Not that there were many women to go around when he was stuck in the backwater swamps of the Mississippi bayous at Stennis where SBT-22 was headquartered.

If he were to pursue a woman, Tracie wouldn't be the one. She was some kind of special agent for Hank Derringer. She didn't have any more time than he had to get involved. Not that they would even be compatible. She was too…

Rip struggled to find the right word.

The tightness of her jaw and the slightly narrowed, beautiful green eyes said it all. Intense.

He'd bet she was just as intense in bed. Again his groin strained against the denim of his jeans. Now was not the time to think about getting naked with a woman. He had a job to do.

As a dead man, he needed to resolve the case so that he could resurface alive before the Navy processed him out of a job.

"We're here," Tracie said as the limo slid up beside the curb in front of what appeared to be a three-star hotel only a few blocks from the airport. "The driver will remain nearby in case we need him on short notice."

Rip nodded and glanced at the hotel. "Once inside, who do we ask for?"

"We don't. We check in as newlyweds." Tracie glanced his way. "You'll need your driver's license and credit card. Our guy is in room 627. We'll make our way up to his room after we check in."

Rip pulled out the wallet Hank had provided and familiarized himself with the contents and his new name. *Chuck Gideon.* "Who came up with the name?"

"Does it matter?"

"No." Rip got out, rounded the vehicle and beat the chauffeur to opening Tracie's door. "Mrs. Gideon, shall we get a room?" He winked and smiled.

Tracie's eyes narrowed slightly and she placed her hand in his, allowing him to pull her to her feet on the pavement.

His fingers tingled where they touched hers, but Rip schooled his expression, determined to give no indication that Tracie had any effect on him.

As soon as she was on her feet, she let go of his hand.

Not to be deterred, and using their married status as an excuse, he rested his hand at the small of her back. A slight tremor shook her body. Inside the lobby of the hotel, Rip adopted his role. "We'd like a room for the night."

"Just a moment, sir." The hotel manager's fingers flew across the keyboard. "We have one suite left on the seventh floor."

"Perfect," Tracie smiled. "We'll take it."

Rip grinned at the manager. "She can't wait to get me alone." He held up her left hand, displaying the diamond ring and wedding band on her finger. Then he held up his left hand, displaying a matching wedding band. "Newlyweds."

The manager smiled and handed them two key cards. "Congratulations."

"Let's wait to get the luggage until we've seen the room," Tracie said, with a flirty bat of her eyelashes.

Though Rip knew it was all part of the act, it didn't stop his pulse from leaping and his blood from thrumming hot through his veins. They stepped into the elevator. Before the door closed, Rip pulled Tracie into his arms and kissed her soundly.

The elevator doors slid shut and Tracie pushed him away, straightening her dress unnecessarily, her hands shaking. "We don't want to look overeager."

"Don't you think newlyweds are anxious to get to their hotel room?"

Tracie shrugged. "I wouldn't know, never having been a newlywed." Her words were tight and it was as if a shutter descended over her green eyes.

"Well, I guess that answers one question."

"Oh, yeah? What's that?"

He smiled, liking that he'd shaken her with his kiss. "You've never been married. So you're not married now."

Turning her back to him, she said, "What does it matter?"

"I would think it would matter a little since we just kissed."

"All part of our cover. It didn't mean anything."

"If you were married, wouldn't you hope that your husband would be a little jealous of the man kissing his wife?"

"I would hope he'd understand it's part of the job. Not that I'm getting married anytime soon."

"Why not?"

"I'm not convinced marriage is all that great."

Having been a SEAL for seven years, Rip had much the same perspective, though he'd never voiced his opinion on the institution. Tracie made him reconsider his own stand on matrimony. "I think marriage is okay for some."

Tracie's lips twisted as she glanced up at him. "But not you?"

He countered with raised brows. "Or you?"

"Marriage is hard enough when the two parties involved live under the same roof all year long. My jobs in the FBI and now on Hank's team have kept me moving. I don't have the time or the inclination to set down roots."

The door opened on the seventh floor. Rip took the lead, turning toward the stairwell instead of the room the hotel manager had assigned them. Tracie was right behind him.

He hurried down the stairs checking for security cameras. He'd seen one in the hallway on the seventh floor, but not in the stairwell. One floor down, he opened the door.

Movement captured his attention. Two men were entering the stairwell at the opposite end of the long corridor. The last one through looked over his shoulder at Rip and Tracie before shoving the guy in front of him the rest of the way through the door and crowding in behind him.

"Damn." Tracie ducked past Rip and ran for room 627. The doorjamb was splintered and the door stood ajar. Tracie pulled a pistol from her purse and shouldered her way inside, gun pointed.

Rip dragged the HK .40 from the holster beneath his shirt and rushed in after Tracie.

"Franks is dead." Tracie turned toward him. "Whoever did it got away."

"The two in the stairwell." Rip ran back to the stairwell. He took the steps two at a time, jumping over the railing as the staircase made a turn. He landed and repeated the process until he hit the ground floor where he burst through the doorway. As dark sedan rushed by, one of its windows lowered and the barrel of a pistol jutted out.

Rip threw himself to the ground as the sharp report of gunfire blasted the air. He rolled beneath a truck and out the other side, jumping to his feet. Another shot shattered the truck's passenger window.

Hunkered low with the body of the truck between him and the fleeing vehicle, Rip sucked in a breath and dared to poke his head over the top of the hood, praying he'd have enough time to get a fix on the license plate of the sedan. Already, it was too far away and getting farther.

Rip ran across the grass, cut through a stand of trees and made it to the street as the getaway vehicle turned onto the main road.

He hammered his pistol's grip into the driver's side window, cracking the glass.

The driver cursed, and the vehicle slowed for a second. Tires squealing, it leaped across the crowded roadway, and three other vehicles crashed into each other as the drivers slammed on their brakes.

With the pileup blocking Rip, the killers got away.

Farther away from Tracie and the scene of the crime than he felt comfortable with, Rip jogged back to the hotel, and raced up the six flights of stairs.

Tracie was still in room 627 with the dead DEA supervisor.

Rip nudged the door open with his foot, breathing hard, his shirt torn and dirty.

"What happened?" Tracie asked.

"They got away." Rip kicked the door closed behind him, careful not to touch anything. "Have you called the police?"

She shook her head and held up gloved hands. "No. And I've been careful not to leave prints on anything. We can't blow our cover. There's still a lot of work to do."

"What about the surveillance video for this floor?"

"I'll get Hank to work on that. Right now, we need to find any information that Greer might have left for us." She slapped a pair of latex gloves in his hands.

Rip pulled on the gloves and glanced around the hotel room. Drawers littered the floor, a small suitcase lay upside down beside the drawers, clothes were strewn around the room as if someone had gone through them in a hurry. Pillows had been tossed off the bed and the mattress lay at an awkward angle, the sheets in a rumpled heap beside the dead man.

"The room's been tossed. If there was anything to be found, don't you think the killers would have gotten to it first?" Rip asked.

He glanced at the door. Not only had the killers splintered the frame, the chain lock had been ripped out of the door itself.

"The chain on the door was torn off. The agent knew someone might try to get to him." Tracie checked the closet, the empty room safe and behind the dresser. "Nothing."

Rip found a set of keys beneath the corner of the bed. "Think he might have left something in his vehicle?"

"We can check, but we better make it quick. It won't be long before someone sees the broken door and discovers the body. We don't want to be around when the police get here."

Rip nodded. They couldn't afford to be tied up answering questions for the police. Their fake documents would only hold up until authorities tracked down their real identities. "Did Hank have the access to erase our fingerprints from the FBI and military databases?"

"As far as I know, he removed us from all grids."

A sense of loss washed over Rip. His identity had been erased from the military system. He'd always been proud of his connection with the SEALs. Having been removed from the system made him feel even more disconnected than his fake death.

Rip squared his shoulders. He didn't have time to grieve his own death. Palming the car keys, he jerked his head toward the door. "Let's go."

# Chapter Three

Leading the way, Rip took the staircase down to the ground level.

Tracie followed more slowly in her high heels, listening for others entering the stairwell or raising the alarm about a killing in the hotel.

So far, nothing had gone according to plan, which was right on par for the life of an FBI agent, or a Covert Cowboys, Inc. operative for that matter. Rarely did she have complete control over what happened, but she'd rather be in the position of giving the orders than taking them. She frowned at Rip's back.

The massive breadth of Rip's shoulders gave her a modicum of confidence. At least he was capable of defending himself and possibly her, if hand-to-hand combat became necessary.

Outside in the parking lot, Rip hit the unlock button on the key fob. A nondescript gray economy car's lights blinked and the vehicle let out a mechanical beep.

Thankfully, the car was parked at the side of the building, not in clear view of the lobby or the hotel manager, and hopefully out of range of security cameras.

Without wasting time, Rip dove into the car and thoroughly searched the interior before he gave up and popped the lock on the trunk. It was empty.

"Check under the mat where the spare tire and tools are located," Tracie suggested.

His hand already skimming over the edges of the trunk lining, Rip found the tab to pull it upward. Beneath the felt-covered liner was a large envelope tucked next to the spare.

A siren sounded in the distance. Tracie's pulse leaped. "Grab it and let's get out of here. We don't know if that siren is headed this way."

Rip grabbed the packet, dropped the car keys on the ground nearby and peeled off the gloves, tucking them into his pocket.

Rip put his arm around Tracie, tucking the package between them as they made their way toward the limousine the driver had parked in the far corner of the hotel parking lot.

With Rip so close, Tracie had a hard time concentrating and she stumbled.

Rip's hand on her arm steadied her. "You all right?"

"I'm fine," she said. "Which is more than I can say for Franks." Before Rip could reach for the back door, the driver hopped out and opened the door for Tracie. Rip helped her into her seat, leaning across to slide the package onto the seat beside her. In the process, he stole a kiss.

Startled by the feel of his lips on hers, Tracie froze, her mouth tingling, her hands pressed to her chest to still her furiously beating heart.

When Rip rounded to the other side of the vehicle and slid in beside her, his jaw tight.

"Was the kiss necessary?" she whispered.

"It was part of our cover," he said, his lips twitching in the corners.

"Well, warn me next time," Tracie muttered.

"Sorry, I thought you'd want me to act like the love-sick bridegroom."

He had a point. He also had her trembling, and that just wouldn't do.

He winked at her and glanced at the driver. "For now, just get us away from the hotel."

The driver nodded and shifted gears, setting the limo into motion.

Rip pressed a button and the privacy window between the driver and the passengers slid upward.

As soon as they were back on the main road and Tracie was certain they weren't being followed, she opened the packet and peered inside.

"What's in it?" Rip cast a quick glance her way.

"Photos and some printouts from the internet." Tracie thumbed through the contents.

"Photos of?" Rip queried.

"People. They appear to be Latino." She handed one to him. The image was at an odd angle, as if whoever had taken it hadn't been focusing on the subject. "This is marked as Juan Villarreal."

Rip's eyes narrowed and a muscle ticked in his jaw. "Villarreal was the leader of the terrorist camp we raided in order to free the DEA agent. He's the one in charge of the group using the US-supplied weapons. The photos are probably more of those taken by Greer while he was embedded. I'm surprised they made it all the way to his boss in the States. I had the feeling the flash drive he gave me before he died was all the evidence he managed to get out. Find anything else?"

"More photos and a hand-drawn map." Tracie pulled the map out of the packet and unfolded it in her lap.

Rip leaned over the map. "Looks like the layout of the camp before we raided. I don't think it will do much good now."

"Maybe not, but the photos might help." Tracie gathered

the information and slid it back into the packet. "We need to get this information to Hank and let him run it through his computers."

"And how will we do that?" Rip asked.

"Back at the airport. Everything we need is on the airplane."

Rip studied the controls on the armrest and hit the one marked mic. "Driver, take us back to the airport."

"Yes, Mr. Gideon," the chauffeur responded.

Tracie shot a brief text message to Hank telling him what had happened and to clear the hotel's video feeds of their images.

They arrived at the hangar within minutes and entered the big space where the airplane sat waiting for them.

An attendant hurried over to them, "We've topped off the fuel and checked all fluid levels. As soon as the chauffeur indicated you were on your way back to the airport, the pilot conducted all preflight inspections and is ready to file a flight plan."

As they approached the aircraft, the steps were lowered. Tracie climbed aboard first, followed by Rip. The flight attendant secured the door behind them. Tracie led the way to the middle of the plane where she flipped one of the tabletops open, revealing a computer screen. She tapped several keys, and in moments she had Hank's face up on the screen. "Hank, we're back on board the *Freedom Flight*."

"Glad you're safely aboard. Brandon wiped the security video of any images including you and Schafer."

"Good. I'm not certain how soon the body will be discovered. Your help with the security footage should give us some time to get out of Atlanta. We found some data in the DEA boss's vehicle. I'm scanning it now."

She raised another part of the table, revealing a computer scanner, and fed the documents they'd found in the DEA agent's vehicle into the machine.

Hank's attention shifted to something beside his monitor. "Got them. I'll have Brandon double check the identities of the men in the photos. But I can't move on nailing the suppliers of the weapons until we have some serial numbers."

Rip frowned and leaned close to Tracie so that he could see and be seen by Hank. "The only way to get serial numbers is to go back to Honduras and get them off the guns."

Hank nodded. "Afraid so."

Rip's gaze captured Tracie's and then returned to Hank. "She can't come with me. It's too dangerous."

Hank's brows rose. "Miss Kosart's a trained professional. She knows the risks."

"Look, frogman, I can speak for myself." Tracie shoved him aside. "I'm on board. So we're headed to Honduras as planned?"

Hank smiled. "You can opt out, if you feel it's too dangerous for your liking?"

"I've been in worse situations," she said, her lips thinning.

"Exactly. You might not want to go to that extreme again. The men in that terrorist camp are pure evil and have little regard for women."

"Hank's right," Rip confirmed. "It's not a good place for a woman."

"Or a man." Tracie crossed her arms. "If we don't go in for the additional information, how will we stop whoever it is selling American weapons to terrorists?"

Rip opened his mouth to say something, but the stubborn set of Tracie's chin made him realize he wouldn't get her to change her mind. Instead, he turned to Hank. "I won't be able to focus on the mission if I'm worried my partner can't keep up or will be captured and tortured."

"She's your partner. We can't activate your SEAL unit and send them in again. They've been in once and that got one of your men killed. Someone is dirty on the Fed side. Until we find that person, we can't count on the secrecy of the operation if we involve your unit or any other government agency."

"I trust my brothers."

"So did Gosling." Hank stared straight into Rip's eyes. "Tracie can handle it."

"Yeah," Tracie said, her ire up. "I don't need you or any other man telling me what is too dangerous for me. We go in together or, if you think it's too dangerous, I'll go alone."

Tracie stared at Rip, holding his gaze, daring him to try to override her decision.

Finally, Rip shrugged. "It's your funeral."

"That plan is not in my books." Tracie aimed for confident, when inside she wasn't quite as certain. The kidnapping in Mexico had shaken her more than she cared to admit.

"Then you're deluding yourself. You're headed right into trouble."

Her chin tilted upward. "That's my choice."

The flight attendant appeared. "If you would fasten your seat belts, we can get underway."

Rip frowned into the screen. "How do you propose the two of us sneak into the terrorist camp?"

"I've got that covered. You will be the guests of a friend of mine." Hank grinned. "You're honeymooners, I'm sure they have tourists wander off the beaten path on occasion. And Rip you will be especially prone to wandering off. Your cover is a wealthy entrepreneur looking for potential investment property."

"On my honeymoon?"

"My contact has the story spreading already. You're

notorious for your arrogance and disregard for anyone but yourself."

Rip snorted. "I'm an entrepreneur in a violent, nearly lawless country?"

Tracie's brows rose. "Are you afraid?"

He met her stare with his own, his lips firmly set into a straight line. "Not for me. If you recall, I've been there. I know what the terrorists are capable of."

"Then you'll be the best guide to get us back in there." Tracie nodded at Hank. "We're good to go."

Hank tipped his head. "Glad to see you two agreeing. Your flight plan has been filed. Brandon tells me you're number three in line to take off. My contact, Hector De-Vita, will greet you on his private landing strip. I'm sending two of my best bodyguards from CCI to provide some backup. They should arrive soon after you."

"Only two?" Rip's lips thinned. "Honduras is overrun with rebels, terrorists and guerillas, and you're sending only two of your best bodyguards for us?"

Hank smile. "DeVita will augment with several men of his own. He's in the security business, providing bodyguards and human shields to the wealthier members of Honduras's population. The plane you're on is fully equipped with an arsenal of weapons you might familiarize yourself with."

Tracie harrumphed. "Some honeymoon."

"Nothing but the best for my baby," Rip winked at her.

"Good luck, you two. Make use of the satellite phone if things get tough. I'll answer at any hour."

When the call ended, Rip stared across at Tracie. "I felt better going in under the cover of dark with my SEAL team."

"What? You're not up for a frontal assault in full daylight with only a girl as your sidekick?" She leaned back in her chair. "No guts, no glory."

The giant hangar door opened to let in the afternoon glare. The plane taxied out into the sunshine. Within minutes, they were in the air, winging their way to Honduras.

Tracie closed her eyes. "You might as well get some rest. Once we hit the ground in Honduras, we'll need all our faculties to pull off this information-gathering honeymoon."

Once they had serial numbers or even a manifest, they might have a chance of tracing the weapons back to those in the United States who had sold them. Nothing like barreling into a potentially hostile situation pretending to be a newlywed couple to get your adrenaline pumping.

Knowing they were headed into a hotbed of danger in the steamy Central American jungles of Honduras didn't stop a chill from slipping across Tracie's skin.

Whatever happened, she refused to be taken captive ever again. If the terrorists wanted her, they'd have to kill her before she'd surrender.

RIP REMAINED AWAKE, studying all the information they had on the case. He reviewed every photograph to glean as much insight as possible from the details in the images they'd obtained from Franks…everything from the faces to the crates of weapons.

After the botched retrieval of the DEA agent by SBT-22, the terrorist camp had probably moved to another location, taking advantage of the jungle's canopy for concealment from satellite photography. Finding them would be a challenge.

Beside him, Tracie had leaned back in the contoured seat with her eyes closed, the steady rise and fall of her chest letting Rip know she'd fallen asleep.

His attention shifted from the computer to the sleeping woman beside him.

Her long, soft brown hair fanned out around her shoulders, and her dark brown lashes made shadowy crescents against her cheeks. Apparently, she was caught in a not-so-pleasant dream. She shivered again and whimpered.

Her eyelids twitched, her eyes beneath them darting back and forth. Her fingers clenched the armrests and a tremor shook her body. Rip motioned to the flight attendant to bring a blanket. He took it from her and laid it across Tracie his hand finding hers.

She let go of the armrest, fingers curling around his, squeezing so tightly she nearly cut off his circulation.

"Tracie," Rip whispered. "Wake up."

Her head turned from side to side and she whimpered again.

"Tracie, wake up." Rip made his entreaty more forceful. He didn't like seeing her in such distress. What kind of dream was it to make her so upset?

When she still didn't wake, he leaned forward and captured her face between his palms. "Tracie, it's okay. You're just dreaming."

The CCI agent's eyes blinked open, the startling green of them piercing Rip through the heart with the anguish reflected in them. She stared around at the interior of the plane. "What...where?" She shook her head and her gaze locked with Rip's.

He stroked his thumbs across her cheek. "Remember me? I'm your husband." He winked and pressed a kiss to her forehead, liking the sound of the word on his lips. What would it be like to be Tracie's husband? "You were having a bad dream." He leaned back, letting go of her face.

Tracie touched her fingers to the place he'd kissed and

frowned. "Oh, it's you." Dragging in a shaky breath, she let it go slowly and sat up. "I'm sorry. For a moment I forgot where I was."

"I take it you weren't in such a good place in your dream." He tucked the blanket in around her sides.

Sitting up, Tracie adjusted her seat to an upright position and pulled the blanket up to her chin, her body trembling. "It was only a dream. How long have we been flying?"

"Two and a half hours."

"That long?" She pushed her hair back from her face and slipped an elastic band around the thick hank, securing it in a ponytail at her nape. "I must have needed the sleep. What about you? Did you rest?"

"I can rest when we solve this case, and I can return to the land of the living."

Tracie's lips twisted. "I know this must be difficult for you to play dead and alive at the same time. Hopefully, we'll get in, get out and the terrorists will be none the wiser."

Rip snorted. "That's what we planned when we went in to get Greer out." He glanced out the window into the clear blue sky. "That's not quite how it worked." Gosling's wife had been devastated when she'd gotten the news of his death. She'd almost lost the baby.

Tracie laid her hand on his arm. "We'll do the best we can. You should get some rest."

He leaned his head back and closed his eyes. "What were you dreaming about when I woke you?"

A long moment of silence stretched between them.

Rip opened one eye.

Tracie stared straight ahead, her face pale and drawn. Finally, she spoke. "I was dreaming about Mexico."

Closing his eye again, he allowed his lips to quirk upward in a wry grin. "I take it you weren't dreaming about a vacation to Cozumel?"

"Not hardly."

Rip opened his eyes.

Tracie had turned her head away and stared out the window. Her back stiff.

"Dreaming about being held hostage by members of a drug cartel?"

She nodded.

Rip slid his hand over hers and gently squeezed her fingers. "I'm sorry."

Tracie turned to stare at where their hands touched. "It happens."

"Yeah, but it's not something you get over that easy. I'd bet you have PTSD."

She shrugged. "What do you do? Give up?" She shook her head. "Not my style." Her hand slipped from beneath his.

Rip's grip tightened before she got away. "Sometimes it helps to talk about it."

"Thanks, but I did enough talking to the FBI shrink." She tugged again and he let go of her hand. "I want to get on with my life, not dwell in the past."

"I get it."

"Perhaps we should look at the weapons Hank sent for our use," Tracie suggested.

The flight attendant cleared her throat. "Mr. Derringer also provided additional clothing, if you'd like to change." She opened a small closet with an arrangement of clothing hung on hangers that included several nice dresses in light colors typical of warm climates, a man's light gray suit and a white linen suit next to it.

"Oh, please," Tracie said. "Wear the white one. It reeks of spoiled, rich playboy."

"I thought I was going for wealthy entrepreneur."

"True, but that white, with your dark hair, will make more of a first impression. Very sexy."

Rip's brows rose and his lips curved upward. "You noticed?"

Tracie shrugged. "I'm an agent. It's my job to notice things."

"Uh-huh."

"Fine." Tracie frowned. "Wear the gray one. I don't care." She disappeared around a curtain at the rear of the plane with one of the dresses.

Though he tried not to, he couldn't help watching Tracie's bare feet beneath the curtain. The red dress pooled on the floor and she stepped out of it, then light yellow filmy fabric puddled on the floor of the plane and Tracie's feet stepped into the middle of it.

Something about her bare feet had Rip's blood singing through his veins at Mach 5. He had the urge to yank the curtain back and feast his eyes on her naked body.

A slow chuckle built in his chest and he nearly laughed out loud at what he expected her reaction would be if he followed his urge. He rubbed his cheek where he guessed she'd slap it. But, damn, it would be worth it. The woman had his insides tied in knots.

Tracie emerged, wearing a beautiful dress that hugged her breasts, emphasizing the ripe, rounded fullness while drawing attention to the narrowness of her tiny waist. The skirt flared out and fell to midthigh. Long legs stretched from what seemed like her chin to her slender feet encased in nude, strappy stilettos. She was pulling her hair up into a sleek French twist, her arms raised, head tucked low.

For a moment, Rip could only stand and stare. When she finally glanced up, she caught him gawking.

Snapping his mouth shut, he took the white suit off the hanger and stepped behind the curtain, coming out when he had the white trousers on, a black button-up shirt, open halfway down his chest and the jacket hooked on his finger and slung over one shoulder.

Tracie stood beside the closet, arms crossed over her chest, a cocky look on her face. When she caught sight of him, her mouth opened as if to say something and closed again without uttering a word. She swallowed hard, the muscles in her throat working. "I—" Her voice came out in a tight squeak. After clearing her throat, she finally managed, "I was right. Damned sexy." Then she turned on her stilettos and marched back into the cabin.

Rip chuckled. If he wasn't mistaken, the woman had been tongue-tied by him in a white suit. Who'd have thought a man in a white suit would have that much of an effect on a woman. He'd have to ask Hank where he'd gotten this one. It would be worth it to invest in something that inspiring. Especially if Tracie thought it made him look sexy.

He returned to the cabin with a wide, satisfied grin on his face.

FOR THE NEXT thirty minutes, Rip and Tracie poured over the racks of rifles, grenade launchers, pistols and explosives with which Hank had seen fit to equip the small armory on the airplane.

Rip tucked a HK .40 caliber pistol in his boot, then he grabbed a nine-millimeter Glock in a shoulder holster and slung it over his shoulders.

The flight attendant stepped up behind him and offered to hold the white linen jacket that went with the tailored white trousers, while he slipped his arms into the sleeves.

Though the sleeves were long, the entire outfit was surprisingly comfortable and cool. Used to heavy battle-dress uniforms, bullet-proof vests and helmets, Rip felt somewhat naked and exposed in the suit.

"Smile. You're supposed to be on your honeymoon without a care in the world." Tracie adjusted the collar of his shirt beneath the jacket and patted his chest. "You look more like a kid in his itchy, Sunday best."

Rip fidgeted. "I'd rather go in with my M4 on automatic."

"Well, we can't. We're honeymooners and guests of Hector, so act like you're in love." Tracie's eyes widened and a smile curled her lips. "Unless you've never been in love." Her brows climbed up her forehead. "You haven't, have you?"

He shook his head. "Haven't had the time. I was a little preoccupied with SEAL training straight out of Navy basic and saving the world one bad guy at a time for the past seven years."

She smiled at him. "Let me guess…it's a tough job, but—"

"—someone has to do it." With one arm, he captured her around the waist and clamped her body against his, his other hand reaching up to cup her face in his palm. "Is this better, *mi amore*?" He bent to claim her lips with his. At first he did it to prove a point, but when her body pressed to his, it triggered a response he wasn't prepared for.

Her arms slid around his neck and her breasts pressed against his chest, he couldn't break the kiss to save his life.

Not until a discreet cough sounded nearby.

Her cheeks flushed, the flight attendant gave him a weak smile. "Sorry, but Hank's on the satellite phone. He wants to talk to you two before we land."

Tracie stepped away and wiped the back of her hand over her mouth. "Tell him we'll bring him up on the computer." She took a seat at the monitor and clicked the keyboard, bringing up a video feed of Hank.

"Tracie, Rip." Hank nodded. "We have a little information on the man called Carmelo Delgado we thought you should know. He's a coffee plantation owner. Though they don't have photos to back it up, the Feds think Delgado is a key player with the rebels. His plantation has never been targeted and he keeps a heavy contingent of gunmen employed to protect his interests. Locals say that he is well-known in Honduras for his ruthless disregard for the law and life and for the way he treats women. Or should I say beats women?"

"Sounds like a nice guy," Tracie said, her voice flat.

"Be careful around him," Hank said. "He's dangerous and he could be one of the rebel leaders."

"We'll keep that in mind. Did you find anything else?"

"I don't know if it means anything, but there is a photo of Senator Craine in San Pedro Sula this year. He's been in several of the Central American countries negotiating trade agreements between the different countries and the US."

"So?" Rip stared at the screen, studying Hank Derringer's face. He didn't look like a billionaire. He looked like a rancher with his weathered skin, shock of white hair and a blue chambray shirt he might wear out to the barn to muck stalls.

"Brandon found a photo of Craine and Delgado at a trade meeting, shaking hands."

"Flight attendant, prepare for landing," the captain said over the intercom.

"We're about to land," Tracie told Hank.

"We're still searching for more clues. If we find anything else, I'll call you on the satellite phone." Hank rang off.

Rip took his seat across the aisle and buckled his seat belt, his mind not on the information Hank had imparted but on the kiss that had left his head spinning and his pulse hammering. She was such a distraction, he was afraid he'd lose focus when he needed it most.

Turning his back on Tracie, Rip leaned toward the window, staring down at what appeared to be a jungle rushing up at them, when in fact they were plummeting toward the treetops.

The adrenaline coursing through his veins spiked at the speed of their descent. He peered closer as the Citation X circled, dropping toward the canopy, slowing as it approached the ground.

A wide slash opened up in the green carpet below, revealing an expansive field with a magnificent hacienda sprawled across a hilltop, its stucco walls painted a pale terracotta and accented with creamy white trim. The place had a dark terra-cotta tiled roof and richly dark wooden doors. A sparkling pool provided a splash of blue with palm trees lining the tiled deck.

To the north of the house stretched a long, level green field of grass with several wind socks along its length. It appeared to be more of a fancy playing field than a beautifully manicured and level landing field.

The Citation kissed the turf, the pilot reversing the thrust to come to a swift stop on the grass-covered landing strip. From all appearances they'd landed in a tropical paradise.

The peace and tranquility of the lush setting was short-lived. As they taxied to a halt, several topless Jeeps, with machine guns mounted on them, exploded out of the tree line headed straight for the Citation.

The pilot's voice sounded over the plane's intercom, "Relax, our host assures us the approaching vehicles are his men coming to greet us and ensure our safety."

Rip frowned, patting the Glock in his shoulder holster. "They don't look like the welcoming committee."

Tracie bit her bottom lip. "I hope they're on our side. I'd hate to take live fire from one of those guns." She peered out her window, her brows furrowed.

Even if they'd wanted to, they couldn't take off again and leave. Not with Hector's men surrounding their plane with weapons pointed at them. Now that they were in Honduras, they were Hector's guests, like it or not.

Perhaps a little danger was just what Rip needed to wipe away the aftereffects of that kiss. One thing was certain, it had left an indelible impression on his lips and his libido. Pretending to be a lusty, loving honeymooner wouldn't be such a burden to bear. Turning off the act at the end of this charade would be an entirely different story.

## Chapter Four

Tracie's heartbeat rattled in her chest and the hum of blood banging against her eardrums seemed louder than the plane's engine. What bothered her most was that it had nothing to do with the fear of landing on a short runway in the jungle or the fact that they were surrounded by big, mean-looking men armed with weapons that could cut them down in seconds.

No, her elevated heart rate had more to do with the one man who'd dared to bend her to his will in a soul-defining kiss that she would not soon erase from her memory.

*Holy hell.*

With her back to him, she pressed her fingertips to her pulsing lips. More than anything, she wanted to ask the pilot to take her back to Texas where she could tell Hank that she wasn't the right person for the job. He could get someone else who would be more professional when playing the part of a happily married woman. Someone who could separate truth from fiction, keep them distanced and remain sane throughout the mission.

Oh, her body had the lusty, newlywed part down. The disconnect came when she reminded herself that this was all a ruse and that when this job was over, there would be nothing else between her and the SEAL. After their mission, the man, with his burly muscles and blue eyes she could fall right into would go back about his business of saving the masses from fates worse than death, and protecting the country's freedom.

She would return to Texas and her next assignment with Covert Cowboys, Inc. Her and Rip's paths would never cross again. What would be the point of a relationship with such a man? Not that there was anything happening between them. They were both playing their parts, nothing more.

*Oy.* Then why was her heart still pounding?

The flight attendant lowered the steps into place and Rip headed for the doorway.

Tracie's gaze followed him as he made his way down the steps, his swagger so sexy it made her belly tighten.

She left her seat and followed, sucking in a deep breath before stepping into the doorway and smiling down at him, slammed with the heat and humidity of the Honduran jungle. She could do this, she thought, reminding herself again that it was just an act.

Rip stood at the bottom of the steps and held out his hand, the white of his smile rivaling the brilliant sunshine. "Come on, sweetheart. Our host is waiting. The sooner we meet with him, the sooner we can start our honeymoon." He winked. "You did bring that sexy teddy you got at the bridal shower, didn't you?"

Her heart stopped in her chest as she stared down at the elegantly handsome SEAL dressed in the white linen suit. God, he looked like a million dollars and the man of every woman's dreams with his darkly tanned skin and megawatt grin.

Squaring her shoulders, she forced a broad smile and took his hand, descending with deliberate slowness to give the appearance of a woman tempting her new husband with a sexy turn of her ankle, ready to enjoy every minute of her honeymoon. "I did, darling. It's on top in my suitcase. As soon as we can get to our room, I'll give you a private viewing of me in it."

Before her stilettos touched the ground, he swept her into his arms and bent her over in a sexy and deeply satisfying kiss that stirred her in a thousand different ways all at once.

When he let her up, she batted at his chest. "Oh, baby, save it for the bedroom."

"Why save it, there's much more where that came from, and besides, I can't keep my hands off you." His fingers slid along her spine, down over her bottom and squeezed, pressing her pelvis to his thick thigh.

Tracie leaned up to nip his earlobe. "What are you doing?" She hissed through a broad, fake smile.

"Playing my part, sweetheart. Playing my part." He bent, captured her beneath the knees and swung her around, her filmy skirt floating out around them. "Where's Senor De-Vita?" he asked the nearest guard.

"You are to come with me." A scary man with heavy brows and a wicked-looking AK-47 Soviet-made rifle jerked his head toward a Jeep similar to those surrounding the plane. The leader didn't wait for Rip or Tracie—he strode to the vehicle and climbed into the front seat.

Rip carried Tracie across the grass and settled her into the backseat. A man stood between the front seat and backseat holding on to the machine gun, his gaze skimming across Tracie's shapely legs.

Tucking her dress around her, Tracie covered as much as she could, then slid the edges of the material beneath her to hold the dress down.

Rip climbed in on the other side of the Jeep. Before he was completely settled, the driver gunned the accelerator, sending the SUV into a tight one-eighty and headed back into the solid wall of jungle. A road appeared in front of them, winding through trees to an imposing gate and an even more imposing concrete fence topped with concertina wire.

A chill rippled along Tracie's spine. The fence and gate looked more like the kind you'd see at a prison compound than at a wealthy man's hacienda in the tropics.

Once they cleared the gate, the trees thinned and opened onto a wide knoll that must have been a good ten acres of manicured lawns. Gracefully designed landscape surrounded the sprawling hacienda with a tall concrete and stucco wall rising up to provide yet another imposing barrier around the owner's home. At least this one didn't sport concertina wire.

As they neared, huge, ornate, steel double doors opened. The Jeep entered the circular driveway and came to an abrupt halt in front of a wide set of elegant stairs, leading up to the glass and wrought-iron entrance.

A man stood at the top of the stairs, dressed similarly to Rip in a white linen suit, white leather shoes and a smoky gray shirt beneath the jacket. A thick gold chain shone through the V of his shirt's neckline, reflecting sunlight off the links.

His hair was full, dark and smoothed back from his forehead, falling to brush the tops of his shoulders. He wore a goatee and his eyes were shiny black. When he smiled, his white teeth shone in stark contrast against his bronze-toned skin.

The Jeep driver shifted into Park, jumped from his seat and circled around to Tracie's side. The man who'd greeted them at the plane climbed out of the Jeep and spoke to the man on the steps in swift Spanish to which the man replied sharply.

Rip took Tracie's arm in a firm grasp and helped her

from the Jeep and then addressed the man on the steps. "You must be Hector DeVita."

Their original welcoming committee and chauffeur backed away from their boss, settled in the vehicle and drove away, leaving Tracie and Rip alone to face their host.

Only they weren't alone. Tracie counted no fewer than four men bearing assault rifles—two positioned at the corners of the front of the hacienda, and two a couple steps behind Hector. All four men were dressed in black trousers and black T-shirts, and they wore sunglasses that hid their eyes.

"*Si*, I am Hector DeVita." The man in white spread his arms wide. "Senor and Senora Gideon, welcome, *por favor. Mi casa es su casa.*" He stepped sideways and waved them up the stairs and past him into the shadow of the entrance. "Hank has told me so much about you. I understand congratulations are in order."

Tracie adjusted inwardly to the use of their fake married name, while smiling politely at Hector. "That's nice since he's told us so little about you. I hope we can rectify that misfortune."

"Certainly," he said. "*Por favor*, step inside. The day is *muy caliente*, and I think a cool drink is much needed."

A servant dressed in a powder-blue guayabera shirt and dark pants opened and held the door.

Tracie stepped inside onto a gleaming white marbled foyer with impossibly high ceilings that created a sense of elegant spaciousness. A sweeping staircase with mahogany railing curved to the right to a second level.

"Your home is lovely," Tracie said.

Hector gave a slight bow. "*Gracias*, Senora Gideon."

"Please, call me Phyllis."

Hector took Tracie's hand and raised it to his lips, pressing a light kiss to her skin. "Phyllis, you are *muy bonita*." He clutched her fingers longer than she liked.

Rip held out his hand to Hector, forcing the man to acknowledge him and release his hold on Tracie. "Nice to meet you, Senor DeVita. You can call me Chuck."

"Chuck." Hector shook Rip's hand and let go. He turned to the interior of the luxurious hacienda and waved a hand toward the staircase. "My servant will show you to your room. Once you have had time for a short siesta, I would be pleased if you would join me for dinner. We get so few visitors here. At that time we can discuss your visit and security needs while you honeymoon in Honduras."

Chuck nodded. "I look forward to dinner." He hooked an arm around Tracie's waist. "But for now, I'd like that siesta. I haven't had two minutes alone with my new wife since the wedding."

Hector's brows rose. "A beautiful woman is not someone to be ignored. If I had such a lovely wife, I would not waste my honeymoon on business."

"Phyllis is not only gorgeous—she's an astute businesswoman and she's as eager as I am to begin our search for additional investment property and businesses." He winked at her.

Though she knew his playful look was all for show, the sparkle in his blue eyes and the way he smiled at her made Tracie's stomach flutter and heat rise up her neck to bloom in her cheeks. "But of course. I love the challenge of finding a diamond in the rough and turning it into something of value. It gives me a thrill every time."

"Were you my wife, I would find other ways to excite you, *mi amore*," Hector said.

Rip's eyes narrowed and his smile slipped as his arm tightened around Tracie. "Make no mistake, I know how to please my wife in *every* way."

"Trust me, I didn't marry him just for his brain." Tracie laid a hand on his chest and stared up into his eyes, channeling every sexy move she'd seen in the movies. "He knows me," she whispered and leaned up on her toes to press a kiss to his cheek. "I am a bit tired from the flight." She looked around, ending the conversation that was becoming more uncomfortable by the minute.

"Of course." Hector snapped his fingers and a young woman in a powder-blue dress with a white Peter Pan collar hurried forward. She executed a little curtsy and said, *"Por favor, sigueme."* With a hand motion for them to follow her, she led the way up the stairs and down a long, wide hallway. Arched windows looked out over the glimmering pool surrounded by palm trees and bright splashes of blooming bougainvillea bushes.

If the entire compound were not surrounded by a high concrete fence, with security guards positioned at each corner and several in between, it could easily be mistaken for paradise. Knowing what lay beyond the walls and hidden in the jungles, or even roaming the streets of the cities, Rip knew Honduras was a country in desperate times. The government had little control over the rebels, the military often siding or collaborating with them in order to stay alive.

They walked in silence to the room Hector had assigned them. The servant opened the door and stepped inside, switching on lights. Calling the space a room was an understatement.

The bedroom alone had more square footage than Rip's entire apartment back in Mississippi. Through an arched doorway was a sitting room with a chaise longue, a desk and a leather executive chair.

The maid spoke in halting English, *"El banjo*—the bathroom is here." She led the way through another arched doorway into a bathroom in stark black and white, the counters solid slabs of white granite, specked with flashes of silver and black.

A huge walk-in shower could have fit six people and sported no fewer than four showerheads. The fixtures were polished, gleaming and sparkling clean. Fluffy white towels lay on the counter and near a tub big enough for two people. Lit candles flickered all around, adding to the sunlight shining through a glass brick wall.

"If you need anything, *por favor*, just ask." The maid backed out of the bathroom.

Rip and Tracie followed her to the door of the bedroom, closing it softly behind the maid.

"Wow," Rip said.

Tracie spun and placed a finger over his lips, then stood on her toes to kiss him, pulling his head down so that she could nibble his ear and whisper, "The entire room could be bugged or monitored by video." Louder, she added, "Kiss me."

Rip obliged, gathering her into his arms. While he kissed her, he closed his eyes halfway, glancing around the bedroom from beneath his eyelids. A trained SEAL, he was used to sneaking into villages, or towns, carrying a healthy array of weapons and explosives. Sometimes he searched for surveillance devices on the exteriors of buildings, but for the most part, finding them hidden in a room was a whole new skill to add to his arsenal.

He ran one hand down her back and cupped her bottom, his other hand pushing the hair off her neck, his mouth following his hand, tasting her skin up to her ear where he nipped her earlobe. "You're the expert. What do we look for?" he breathed into her ear.

She winked at him and then turned her back. "Unzip me, please." Tracie pulled her hair aside allowing him access to the zipper.

His heart leaped and he stared down at her. While he would love to get naked with the beautiful former FBI agent, what had made her come around to the idea so quickly? Especially considering the added probability of their movements being recorded.

She spun around, smiled and whispered between her teeth, "Just do it." Giving him her back again, she waited, holding her hair up.

While he obliged, his knuckles skimming across the silky, soft skin of her lower back, Rip tried to keep his mind off the scent of her shampoo, the curve of her shoulders and the flare of her hips.

Forcing his mind away from what he was finding inside Tracie's dress, he stared around the room, checking corners, wall sconces and the chandelier hanging at the center of the room. His breath hitched. At the same time he skimmed the soft, rounded curve of her bottom beneath her dress, he caught sight of a small black device attached to the wrought-iron chandelier.

*"Got one,"* he said softly as he reached the end of the zipper.

Tracie turned and let the dress slide off her shoulders. "Where would you like to begin?" she said loud enough to pick up on any listening device in the room.

Rip's stomach flipped. Hell, he'd like to begin at her lips and taste every inch of body. Unfortunately, she was talking about the location of the camera he'd found.

The yellow dress fell to the floor, pooling around her feet. Wearing nothing but her bra and panties, she batted her eyes, lifted the filmy garment in her hand and paused. "Aren't you going to get undressed?"

"You don't have to ask me twice." He took the dress from her hands and tossed it in the air. The fabric caught on the wrought iron of the chandelier, effectively blocking the view from the miniature camera perched there.

Standing at the bedroom door, Rip switched the light off, to keep the dress from getting too hot on the lightbulbs and catching fire.

Moving quickly and efficiently, Tracie slipped into a silk robe that had been left on the bed. Then she made her way around the room checking behind the wall sconces, beneath the edges of the furniture, inside vases and behind the king-size bed's headboard. When she skimmed her fingers along the underside of the nightstand, she came across another device and pulled it from its mooring.

Rip followed suit, combing over the sitting room and the bathroom, discovering a camera and a listening device in each. Over the cameras, he tossed hand towels. The listening devices he pulled free from the furniture where they were mounted.

Collecting the one Tracie had found, he wrapped them tightly in one of the fluffy towels and stuffed them into the back of a drawer. If the listeners were concerned about the sound being muffled…too bad.

Rip didn't relax until they'd completed a thorough search of the room and Tracie stopped in front him. "I think we got most of them," she said quietly. "But don't let your guard down."

Nodding, Rip sighed. "I don't know about you, but I could use a shower and that siesta."

Tracie smiled. "I'm a bit tired after the flight and everything else. You can go first."

Speaking louder, Rip offered, "Sweetheart, it's our honeymoon, we can shower together." Then he cupped the back of her head and kissed her neck. "Just in case we missed some."

Tracie wrapped her hand around the back of his head. "I'm not showering with you."

His lips trailed across her jawline and back to her earlobe. "I promise not to look."

"Or touch?" she asked.

He raised three fingers. "Scouts honor."

Tracie's brows furrowed. "Why do I get the feeling you've never been a Boy Scout?"

"Probably because I never have." He turned her away and patted her silk-covered behind. "Now go get the water warmed up. I like my showers like I like my women, hot and wet."

Tracie's gasp and the frown she tossed over her shoulder at him made him chuckle. Her cheeks flushed a healthy pink and her eyes flared. He gave her a head start of thirty seconds and then joined her in the bathroom.

Tracie had the shower water running and her silk robe hung on a hook outside the tiled walls of the large walk-in shower.

Rip studied the mirror. Call him paranoid, but he couldn't be certain the mirror wasn't hiding another camera, given the amount of surveillance devices they'd taken from the room.

He told himself he was playing a part. Hank had said from the time they touched ground in Honduras until they left, they had to be completely convincing, even with his contact, Hector. He wasn't absolutely certain of his allegiance to Hank or his alliances with the rebels in Honduras. But he was the best provider of security in the area, with a reputation that had made him a very wealthy man.

For the sake of the mission, Rip shed his white suit and hung it on another hook before stepping into the huge, stone-tiled shower.

Tracie stood with her back to him, her long brown hair

covered in soap suds that slid down her slim athletic, naked body, big suds slipping off the rounded globes of her bottom.

As quickly as he stepped into the shower, he slipped behind her, and clamped one hand around her waist and the other over her mouth.

# Chapter Five

When thickly muscled arms wrapped around her waist, Tracie slammed an elbow backward and stomped her bare heel into the instep of her attacker.

Rip bit down on his tongue to keep from yelling out loud, and let out a pained hiss. "Damn it, it's me."

Her body went rigid, the shower pelting her skin and Rip's face as he leaned close. "I wasn't sure if the mirror might be two-way or hiding a camera. So I got in the shower like we're a newlywed couple." He dropped his hand from her mouth, but didn't loosen the arm around her waist until he was certain she wouldn't attack him again.

Her hands crossed over her breasts and she hunched her shoulders. "Then why did you grab me?"

"I knew I'd startle you and didn't want you to scream."

Tracie snorted. "You got the first part right. Now let go of me and turn around. It's not like we have to take this charade all the way."

"I'll let go if you promise not to hit me again." He groaned. "I think you broke one of my ribs."

"I'm not making any promises or apologies," she said.

He let go anyway and stepped back, admiring her body, before he turned away with equal twinges of guilt and regret.

Switching one of the other showerheads on, he squirted

a handful of body wash into his palm from a dispenser on the wall and rubbed it into his hair and over his shoulders. It was too flowery for his liking, but he imagined it was some high-dollar brand used exclusively by the rich. He preferred a plain bar of soap.

Tracie cleared her throat behind him. "This is awkward."

Rip glanced over his shoulder and caught her looking over hers. He grinned and gave her his back again. "You obviously haven't been in the military. Modesty is the least of your worries." He spoke low enough his voice wouldn't carry outside the shower walls or over the sound of the running water.

"I suppose bullets rank higher on your scale of concerns."

"Yup."

"I guess you had a point. I just wish you'd warned me before we both got in the shower."

"I didn't think about the mirror."

"It's probably just that—a mirror."

"Better safe than sorry."

Tracie snorted.

"By the way," Rip hesitated. "You have a beautiful body." He smiled, knowing his words would get to her.

He wasn't disappointed by the gasp behind him. His smile broadened until he was hit in the head with a sopping washcloth.

"Hey." He turned and grabbed her around the waist as she pulled her arm and the cloth back for a second attack. "I just call it as I see it."

"You weren't supposed to see it." She struggled to free herself from his hold. "Let go."

"Not until you quit swinging at me." The more she wiggled, the more Rip became aware of her rounded, wet breasts pressing against his chest. Before he could will his natural reaction away, his body responded, his groin tightened and his member hardened, pressing into her tight belly.

Tracie froze. "Uh." She bit down on her lip. "Is that what I think it is?"

"Did I mention that I think you have a beautiful body?" He started to set her away from him, but her arms wrapped around his waist holding him against her.

"This is really awkward," she whispered, her voice breathy.

"I'll just leave the shower. You can have it to yourself." He didn't want to leave at all but was afraid that the longer he stayed, the more he'd want to do more than was strictly necessary to nail the role.

"Don't move. I'm naked." Her eyes were round and her cheeks bright pink. And damned if she wasn't biting her lip again.

It was bad enough her naked body was pressed flush against his, but biting that lip did all kinds of crazy to him. It wouldn't take much and he'd be beyond his ability to control himself. And for Tracie's sake, he needed to maintain his control.

Trying not to breathe too deeply and add more friction to the movement between their chests, Rip suggested, "How about I close my eyes and back away."

"Please don't move," she repeated, sounding as if she couldn't get enough air into her lungs.

He reached up and pushed a wet hank of hair out of her face, that little bit of movement making him even more aware of every inch of her skin touching his with the shower's spray heating the space between them. "If I don't move now..." Rip ground his teeth together, his fingers curling around her arms, preparing to push her away. To hell with the possibility of a camera behind the mirror. He couldn't take much more and not...

"What?" Her hands slid up his back.

"What, what?" he said, his mind a blank, all his blood rushing south to another extremity.

"What will happen if you don't move?" She sucked in a breath and let it out slowly, as if it gave her strength and permission to continue to hold him. "You feel it, don't you?" she asked, her words barely above a whisper.

He leaned his head back, letting the shower's spray pelt the back of his head, trying to beat sense into him, one drop at a time. "I feel, a whole lot of you, rubbing against me." He straightened, his grip tightening on her arms. "And it's making me crazy."

"Uh-huh." She nodded. "Same here."

That made him give her a double take. "So what are we going to do about it?"

She shrugged, her breasts rubbing up and down on him. *Sweet Jesus.* She was killing him.

"There's only one thing we can do."

"Yeah? Then tell me. I've never been good at guessing what goes on in a woman's mind. And will you make it quick? I'm about to come undone."

"This." She wrapped one hand around his neck and pulled his head down so that she could press her lips to his. "And this." Her other hand slid down his back to his buttocks, cupping him and pressing him closer. "You see, I figure there's a physical attraction here."

"You think?" He groaned, let go of her arms and skimmed his hands down the curve of her waist. He trailed his fingers over the swell of her hips and cupped the backs of her thighs. In one smooth motion, he lifted her, wrapping her legs around him, pressing her back against the tiles. "What was your first clue?"

"The kiss." She brushed her mouth across his. "Maybe

if we get the elephant in the room out of the way once and for all, we can concentrate on what's more important."

"I like the way you think." He positioned her over his swollen member, ready to drive the point home.

Tracie's hands on his shoulders pressed down and she hovered over him. "One thing…"

His heart hammering against his chest, adrenaline and lust raging through his veins, Rip could barely hear her through the blood pounding in his ears. "What thing?"

"Protection?" she said. "I don't suppose you have some?"

His body on fire, his brain disengaged, it took a moment for Rip to realize what she was saying. "Damn."

"Damn you have to stop to get it or damn you didn't bring any?"

"Damn to both." He buried his face in her neck and moaned. "I had some in my old wallet. Not in the new one."

"This bathroom has just about everything a guest could want…you don't suppose…"

Rip set Tracie on her feet and dove out of the shower, nearly slipping on the tiled floors. Trailing water everywhere he stepped, he riffled through the drawers one at a time.

One had extra washcloths, another had an array of bath salts. Still another had unopened tubes of toothpaste and individually wrapped toothbrushes. When he'd just about given up, Rip opened the bottom drawer in the farthest cabinet and found a supply of lubricants in every flavor imaginable and at least two-dozen foil packages.

He was back in the shower carrying his prize, his ardor no less urgent.

But Tracie had the washcloth draped over her front, barely covering the important parts.

Rip sighed. "Nothing like an important interruption to kill the mood, right?"

She shook her head. "No. I'm perfectly prepared to go through with this." Letting the washcloth fall to the floor, she stepped forward, holding out her hand. "Let me. I'm sure that as soon as we get this over with, we won't be nearly as distracted."

Rip held the packet out of her reach. "You make this sound like the cure to a disease."

"Well, in a way, it is. Once we…do it…it will take away the mystery and we won't be thinking about what it might be like. We can get on with our purpose for being here without unnecessary distraction."

He could see where her thoughts were headed, but her logic was faulty. Once they consummated their relationship, it would only be the beginning. He already knew he'd want more. By the look on Tracie's face, she thought this would be the end and they'd put their physical attraction for each other to bed, so to speak.

Tracie propped her hand on her hip, a worried frown denting her forehead. "Don't you want to have sex?"

Water ran over her shoulders and dripped off the tips of her dusky rose nipples.

Oh, yeah, he wanted it.

He had to clear his throat to answer. "Yes, I do." His member couldn't get any harder. "But, honey, this won't stop here."

"It has to. We are consenting adults with jobs that take us to the ends of the earth. Most likely we won't see each other again. Besides, I'm not interested in anything more than a one-night stand."

A spike of anger jolted through Rip. "Isn't that the man's line?"

"I've been there. Once the lust fades, all you have is regret, and both individuals looking for a way out without hurting the other."

Though he wanted her, Rip knew this was all wrong. "Baby, I don't know who hurt you in the past, but that's not how it works with me." He stepped back, turned and left the shower and her in it.

A sloppy, wet slap sounded behind him and he spun to find a wet washcloth on the floor near his feet. Grumbling echoed inside the shower.

Let her stew. He had some thinking of his own to do. And his thoughts were clearer away from her.

TRACIE STOOD IN the shower, steaming hotter than the water. What just happened? She'd given the SEAL permission to make love to her with no strings attached, demanding no promises for the future. Most men would grab at that opportunity and accept what she was offering, no hesitation.

Not Rip.

She wanted to rant and rave and throw a whopping temper tantrum like a five-year-old deprived of her favorite doll. Only she wasn't five, and she had been all lathered up and ready for some hot and heavy sex. Frustrated beyond anything she'd ever felt she turned the handle on the faucet. Cold water sluiced over her body. Her breath caught in her throat and she shivered, but remained standing in the cool water until the heat of her desire chilled and she could think beyond the sight of Rip's rippling muscles and stiff erection.

Damn. What was wrong with the man?

Or was it her? He didn't desire her enough to take her up on her offer? No, he'd been just as turned on by her as she was by him.

She shut off the water and peeked around the corner of the shower stall. The bathroom was empty of the man she couldn't get out of her thoughts.

Quickly drying off, she slipped her arms into the robe

and pulled it over her body, cinching the belt around her middle before gripping the door handle. Sucking in a deep breath, she squared her shoulders, determined not to show any of her disappointment over Rip's blatant rejection.

Pulling the door open, she stepped through, her chin tilted at a slight angle, determined not to show any emotion to the man.

Tense and slightly hesitant, she stepped out of the bathroom into the bedroom, her belly tight. Her breath caught and held.

The room was as empty as the bathroom. Rip had left.

All the air left her lungs, and a deep sense of disappointment washed over her. Good grief. Had she scared him so badly he'd tucked his tail and run from the room? Wow. Way to shoot a girl down.

Her ego completely deflated, Tracie flopped on the bed, wearing the silk robe and nothing else. Maybe if Rip came back soon, he'd rethink his refusal, part the edges of the robe and take her.

Her heartbeat kicked up a notch and her breathing quickened. Every time she heard a noise, she hoped it was coming from the hallway. At one point she heard footsteps on the tiles outside her door. They paused. She held her breath in eager anticipation, her groin tightening, her body tense.

Then the footsteps moved on.

Releasing the breath she'd been holding, Tracie rolled to her side, tucked her hand beneath her cheek and closed her eyes. If she wasn't going to get the sex she needed to slake her appetite for the man, the least she could do was rest up. She didn't know when they'd head out of the compound in search of the rebel fighters…er…investment property, but she wanted to be ready when they did. Rip had warned her that the guerilla fighters were dangerous and would prefer to shoot first and question later.

She lay with her eyes closed, willing herself to sleep, but the scene in the shower keep replaying against the backs of her eyelids. If she'd kept her mouth shut, she'd be in the middle of what she guessed might have been the best sex of her life.

Rip would be a superb lover. Rough but gentle, aware and insistent on satisfying her needs, the complete opposite of her former fiancé.

She'd met Bruce Masterson on the job when she'd been an FBI special agent. They'd worked a case together and Tracie had been infatuated with him. Still fairly new as an agent, she'd looked up to the man who had several more years experience than she did.

Unfortunately, she'd mistaken infatuation for love and had agreed to marry the bastard before she realized he was linked with one of the deadliest and most traitorous men smuggling drugs and trafficking women and children into the United States: their regional director.

She'd been so blind to their deception, trusting them because they were on her team—supposedly the good guys.

Sadly, Bruce had never loved her. Their engagement had only been a front to help hide his nefarious activities. His deception had cost Tracie her ability to trust men.

Hank Derringer was the exception. If not for him and Covert Cowboys, Inc., she'd be dead. Their relentless pursuit of her and her captors saved her life. But the knowledge that the people she'd worked so closely with in the FBI had been rotten to the core had shaken her to the foundation of her beliefs.

Aside from Hank and the agents he'd assembled in CCI, Tracie didn't know who to trust. That lack of faith in humanity had led to her decision to leave the FBI and go to work for Hank, seeking truth and justice when the police, FBI, military, CIA or other government agencies couldn't seem to get it right or had their hands tied by the powers that be.

She wanted to trust Rip. Admittedly, he was slowly winning her over. After Bruce's betrayal, she'd vowed never to trust another man with her heart. Perhaps that's why she'd spoken up when she did and told Rip that a one-night stand was all she wanted. She was teetering too close to the edge with Rip as it was.

Sleep was the farthest thing from her mind. Instead of lying in the bed, moping about failed relationships and her lack of trust in humanity, she should be up, celebrating a near miss. If she'd made love to the man, she might have broken her vow to herself.

Tracie flopped onto her back and stared up at the high, coffered ceiling with the ornate chandelier hanging at the center, her yellow dress draped across a hidden camera. Her heart beat strong and steady and her mind lurched forward to the task at hand. Since sleep wasn't coming, she might as well get up and get moving.

First thing on her list was to learn more about Hector DeVita and his fortified compound. If he was an ally, good. She'd know what he had available to her and Rip in their quest to find the rebel hideout. If he turned out to be shady, then she'd at least know what they were up against.

## Chapter Six

When Rip left Tracie in the shower, he knew Tracie would think he'd run away. So be it. As a SEAL, he didn't have much time at home. Why waste it on people who didn't give a damn about him? When he was not out fighting battles, he wanted to feel emotionally safe and surrounded by people who cared for and meant something to him.

In the short time he'd known Tracie, he'd come to respect her and he couldn't deny his attraction to her. But one-night stands weren't his style.

His buddies might jump at the chance, claiming life was too short to pass up an opportunity to get lucky. But that was why Rip made every connection count. And he suspected a connection with Tracie would be worth the effort to make it real. Hopping in the sack to get sex out of the way wouldn't make him forget her, or forget what they might have between them.

In the bedroom, he found that, while they'd been in the bathroom, their suitcases had been offloaded from the plane, the clothing unpacked into the dressers or hung in the walk-in closet. He checked to see if the staff had found the wadded up towels stuffed in the back of the drawer. The towels were gone, along with the devices. Damn, they were efficient and, if Hector hadn't figured out before they'd removed the equipment, he'd know now.

Rip selected a pair of light gray trousers and a white button-up shirt—he left three buttons unbuttoned at the top. Still aroused by his naked encounter with Tracie, he didn't want to further tempt himself by being there when she emerged. Slipping into a pair of expensive loafers, he left the room, pulling the door closed.

Out in the spacious hallway, he looked back the way they'd come and turned his back, choosing to search the path yet untraveled. He wandered down the hallway and pushed through a door that led out onto a terrace overlooking a large, beautifully designed infinity pool with water running over the edges in a continuous, soothing flow.

"Join me, Senor Gideon," Hector called out from below.

For a moment, Rip didn't respond, not recognizing the use of his fake name. When he realized Hector was talking to him, Rip descended a set of wrought-iron stairs to the patio surrounding the pool.

The Honduran sat at a bistro table, an iced drink in his hand. "Can I offer you a drink?"

"Yes, thank you. Whatever you're having will be fine."

Hector waved a hand and a servant appeared. He gave the man instructions in Spanish and the servant hurried off. With a smile he faced Rip. "My staff informs me you found my surveillance equipment." He tipped his head. "Well done."

"I like my privacy, even when I'm enjoying the accommodations of my host."

Again, Hector smiled like a gracious host. "I understand perfectly. I hope you did not take offense."

"Not at all," Rip responded.

"Where is the lovely Senora Gideon?"

"She was tired after the flight and chose to sleep through the hottest part of the day."

"And you don't find her company...stimulating enough to lie down with her?"

The servant appeared at that moment with a drink on a tray. He set it down in front of Rip and walked away.

Rip raised the glass and drank, then set the glass on the table. The alcohol took the bite off his irritation with Hector's questions about Tracie. "Jack and Coke. Perfect."

Hector's lip lifted on one side, in recognition of Rip's attempt to steer him away from personal questions. Their host lifted his own drink and held it up. "To your beautiful bride."

Raising his glass Rip tapped it to Hector's. "To my wife. She's an amazing woman, and she's mine." He stared hard over his glass at the man across from him.

His host raised his other hand and chuckled. "How is it you say? Message received?"

Rip relaxed against the back of his chair. "Hank didn't tell us much about you, only that you were a shrewd businessman, the best in security in Central America and somewhat of a ladies' man."

Hector shrugged, the movement smooth and elegant. "I am a rich man. There are many women who would be happy to be with me. But it is rare to find one who isn't interested in only my money."

"And you think Phyllis isn't interested in my money?"

His head canted to the side as Hector considered Rip's question. "It is said that the eyes are the window into a woman's soul. Your wife loves you. She may not know yet how much she does, but it is clear."

*If only.* Rip bit down hard on the inside of his mouth to keep from blurting out that he didn't have her love and he wasn't in love, though the thought of loving Tracie appealed to him. Not many women would understand the life he led.

Having been assigned to different tasks all over as an

FBI agent, Tracie was aware of what it was like to be away from home for long periods of time. Some women wouldn't understand when he couldn't come home for months at a time. Tracie would. Hell, she might be out on assignments of her own.

But what was he thinking? When they had the information they needed and traced the weapons sales back to their source, this gig was up.

His belly tightened.

He'd go his way. Tracie would go hers.

Rip leaned forward. "Hank said he was sending two bodyguards to accompany us while we're out looking at potential properties."

Hector nodded. "He informed me of his plan. He also said you might need more protection and to provide for you only the best and to bill him. I've set aside four of my most trusted men to accompany you. If you like, I can go with you, as well."

Rip held up his hand. "I wouldn't want to take you away from your day-to-day operations."

"It is no problem. I grow bored sitting in my little oasis. So tell me. What is it you're looking for?"

Having done a little research, Rip leaned forward like an eager entrepreneur. "I'm interested in owning my own coffee plantation." Drawing on the satellite images Hank's tech guy had sent plus his own knowledge of the area in question, he proceeded. "My sources told me that there is a coffee plantation near the small town of Colinas Rocosa. From what I've read, they've been successful with rudimentary irrigation techniques. I want to see their operation and the land surrounding it for the potential to expand."

Hector's eyes narrowed. "I am familiar with that area. Carmelo Delgado is the owner that plantation, and it is surrounded by jungle and a river. I seriously doubt Senor

Delgado will sell. The plantation has been in his family for a very long time. It is also a very dangerous area. *Los Rebeldes del Diablo* are known to run the land. I can show you other coffee plantations not nearly so close to trouble."

Rip shook his head. "The other areas are far more expensive. If I can get this coffee plantation at the price I want, I can afford to expand operations."

"Can you afford to pay *Los Rebeldes del Diablo* to keep them from killing you or your workers?"

Pretending to consider Hector's words, Rip tipped his head to the side and touched his chin. "You run a security firm. I could hire your services to protect my interests."

Hector shook his head. "I provide bodyguards for wealthy business owners and their families. I install expensive surveillance equipment in warehouses, stores and homes. I am not equipped to guard entire plantations against *Los Rebeldes del Diablo*. They are an army unto themselves."

"If you won't do it. I'll take care of it myself."

"How?"

"I'll hire mercenaries to stand guard over the land." Rip narrowed his eyes. "Or I'll pay the tithe to *Los Rebeldes del Diablo*. In the meantime will you provide the bodyguards I need to protect me and my wife so that we can get to the plantation?"

"Surely, you are not considering taking your wife with you? It is suicide."

"My wife is quite aware of the dangers. She has a gun and knows how to use it."

"Then not only will she be in danger of attacks by *Los Rebeldes del Diablo*, but if she is caught by the authorities carrying a weapon, she will be thrown in jail." Hector held up a hand. "Honduran jails are no place for Senora Gideon."

"Did I hear my name?" Tracie stepped out of the house onto the tiled decking.

Rip noted she wore thin, harem pants in a pale cream and a silky watermelon-pink blouse that draped her breasts and tiny waist, emphasizing her curves rather than hiding them. Rip's pulse picked up and his fingers clenched into a fist to keep himself from reaching out to her.

Hector stood and pulled a chair out for her, pushing it in as she settled on the cushion. "You did. I was just enlightening your husband on the dangers of traveling in the countryside."

"Are the guerillas still active in this area?" Tracie asked.

Hector nodded. "You did take note of the fences and concertina wire you had to pass through to get here, did you not? These precautions are necessary to protect what is mine."

"We are prepared to take the risk." Tracie smiled at their host and leaned back in her chair, crossing one slender leg over the other. "Hank is sending two of his best bodyguards."

Hector's jaw hardened. "It won't be enough."

"Hank said that you would augment our protection with whatever else we would need. And we'll need transportation, too."

A muscle in Hector's jaw ticked. "I can provide the SUVs and four men to escort you. I advise you to travel in the daylight and not linger too long in one place. If you don't announce that you are coming, you have a better chance of getting in and out without being accosted." Hector waved his hand. "Unless, of course, *Los Rebeldes del Diablo* have checkpoints set up on the roads. In which case, you should turn around and get out of there as fast as you can."

Tracie inhaled and slowly released the breath… "Understood."

His lips thinning into a straight line, Hector snarled. "You may *think* you understand. These men are ruthless.

They cut down a woman and a six-year-old child while I watched helplessly from my office window in Tegucigalpa."

Tracie laid a hand over Hector's. "I'm so sorry."

Though Rip could appreciate her compassion, he didn't like the way Hector turned his hand upright and gripped Tracie's. But he held his tongue.

Hector continued, his head down, his gaze where his hand held Tracie's. "They are ruthless and have no regard for life, and no remorse. All they know is how to threaten and follow through with their threats by killing anyone who crosses their paths."

"Why don't the people rise up against them?"

"The guerillas are armed. The citizens of Honduras are not. And the citizens value the lives of their loved ones. If they try to fight against the guerillas, *Los Rebeldes del Diablo* steal their wives, husbands and children and kill them or hold them for ransom."

"That's terrible." Tracie's brows tugged together.

"So you see, if you want to look at a coffee plantation, I implore you—look somewhere else. Perhaps another country."

Rip leaned back, his arms crossing over his chest. "I know I can make this work. I'm not afraid of the *Diablos*."

"You should be." Hector shifted his gaze to Tracie. "If not for your own sake, then for your wife's."

Tracie smiled reassuringly. "Chuck will protect me. I'm sure we will be okay surveying the plantation. After all, we'll go during the daylight and return here before dark."

"*Los Rebeldes del Diablo* do not confine their terror to the shroud of darkness. They have been known to walk into a restaurant or café in the middle of the day and kill everyone in it."

"Then we will stay out of restaurants. Tomorrow Chuck and I want to see *le Plantación de Ángel* coffee plantation."

With a sigh, Hector stood. "I can see that you are not to be dissuaded. I will inform my men that they will ride with you or follow you to the plantation and remain there until you return."

"Thank you, Hector." Tracie glanced at the man. "I can only imagine the anguish you felt at witnessing the deaths of that mother and child. It's such a senseless act to kill innocents."

Hector slowed on his way back into the house and turned again to face them. "Honduras is my home, but sometimes I hate it so much I wish to leave. I will have my assistant make arrangements for your visit to the plantation. Hank's bodyguards are scheduled to fly in tonight. I will not be at dinner, but my staff will see to your meal. Dinner is served at seven." He didn't wait for a response, disappearing inside the house.

TRACIE STARED AFTER the owner of the hacienda, her heart tight in her chest. "He could be right. Perhaps it is too dangerous to go in broad daylight."

"I want to see how many eyes and ears are employed by the rebel leader and how far out they are stationed," Rip said. "We need to know where they get their groceries and supplies. In order to find out where those boxes full of weapons came from, we have to find members of the *Diablos* and follow them back to their camp."

"Yeah, but wouldn't it be better to sneak in under cover of nightfall and do the same?"

"They will have moved from their last location after our attempt to extract the DEA agent. We don't have their coordinates and, most likely, they've chosen a well-concealed spot in the jungle, beneath the canopy and out of view of our satellites."

"Couldn't you get satellite images that show heat signatures?" Tracie asked.

"I'm sure military intelligence is working on it, but there are miles and miles of jungle out there to scan. In the meantime, we could have already found the camp, located a name and traced it back to whoever is selling the weapons to them."

Tracie sighed. "Then we do it."

As they'd been talking, the sun had been steadily sliding toward the horizon, the shadows lengthening. Lights came on in the pool and a servant worked his way around the patio, lighting tiki torches. The atmosphere became more and more intimate as the sky darkened.

Alone with Rip, Tracie couldn't help but feel uncomfortable about her attempt to seduce him in the shower. Apparently he was not nearly as attracted to her as she was to him, or he would have taken her up on her offer, no questions asked.

With desire flaring up in the pit of her belly, Tracie leaned forward, prepared to run. "If you'll excuse me, I think I'll go change into something more formal for dinner."

As she started to rise, a hand halted her progress.

"Just to make things clear," Rip whispered. "I would have made love to you."

She tried to pull away, her cheeks heating with embarrassment. Had he read her mind? "I know a brush off when I hear it."

His grip tightened and he gave a quick yank, forcing her to fall forward to land in his lap.

"That's better." He nibbled at her ear, while whispering, "Now we look like a newlywed couple and you have proof that I find you extremely attractive."

The hard ridge beneath the placket of his trousers nudged

her bottom and a thrill shivered across her body. Oh, yes, he was attracted. "Then why walk away?"

His hand clamped on either side of her face, forcing her to look him in the eyes. "Because you're a smart, beautiful and wonderful woman, and you deserve more than a fleeting affair." He leaned closer, brushing his lips across hers. "And I mean to show you how much more you deserve than a one-night stand." His words were low, his breath warm against her lips and then he crushed her to his chest, his mouth claiming hers.

Unable to resist, Tracie wrapped her arms around his neck and gave in to the desire that had been building since she'd first met this incredible man.

His tongue slid along hers in an urgent caress, drawing a heartfelt moan from deep in her chest. Warm, strong hands slipped down her back and up her sides, his thumbs skimming the underside of her breasts.

So caught up was she in his seduction, Tracie didn't hear anything outside her own moans and the blood pounding against her eardrums.

Rip raised his head, reluctantly releasing her lips.

The man she'd first seen wearing the powder-blue servant uniform when she'd entered the hacienda stood ten feet away, his head downcast but peering up from beneath heavy black brows. When he was certain he had their attention, he spoke quietly, "Pardon, Senor, Senora. Dinner will be served in fifteen minutes."

"Thank you," Rip said without releasing his hold on Tracie's body.

After the servant left, Rip stared into Tracie's eyes. "That's just a taste of what you could have."

Her body on fire, Tracie wanted nothing more than to retreat to their room and make mad, passionate love to this man. But there was more than sexual desire emanating from his eyes. He held her gaze with an intensity she could imagine he used to attack any challenge, including taking on the enemy. "Just so you know, I'm not good at relationships. Bruce, my ex-fiancé is a perfect example of how lousy I am at it. I don't think he was really ever interested in me to begin with."

"Then your fiancé didn't deserve you." He dragged in a deep breath and let it out. "I guess I have more work to do on that front." His hands wrapped around her hips and lifted her off his lap to stand on her feet.

She wobbled for a moment, still affected by that kiss.

"Go, change into something more formal. I'll see you at dinner." He turned her and patted her bottom, propelling her forward.

Torn between being annoyed and flattered, she thought about slapping him for patting her fanny. Instead, she chose to scurry away before she threw herself into his arms and begged him to take her back to the room, not send her back on her own.

Tracie entered through the back patio door and turned down a wide, airy hallway, heading for the wing where their room was located.

Halfway down the hallway, Hector stood staring at a portrait.

Her feet making very little noise, Tracie was almost to Hector before he noticed her.

He stiffened and stepped back.

Tracie glanced at the portrait of a woman and a small boy and it hit her.

Hector had witnessed the murder of a woman and a small boy at the hands of the guerilla fighters.

A lead ball dropped to the pit of her stomach and her eyes burned with unshed tears. "These are the woman and child you were talking about, aren't they?"

He didn't respond at first, a muscle ticking in his jaw. Finally, he nodded. "I had known Marisol since we were both children. She had such a hard time getting pregnant. When Alejandro was born…" Hector broke off, scrubbing a hand through his dark hair. "I'd never seen her happier."

"You must miss them terribly."

Hector nodded. "I'd give anything to have them back."

"I imagine you would."

He closed his eyes and seemed to draw himself up before he turned to her. "Hank did not tell me why you and your husband really came to Honduras. It is not a honeymoon getaway for most people."

Having just witnessed Hector's raw emotions about the loss of his wife and son, Tracie was tempted to blurt out the real reason they were there. But she bit down hard on her tongue, remembering Hank's entreaty not to trust anyone, even his contact.

Tracie shrugged. "In case you haven't figured it out, Chuck and I love a challenge. We like adventure and working through difficult situations. It's what makes our relationship so exciting." *Among other things*, she added silently.

Hector held her gaze for a long moment before nodding. "Very well. If you have other goals in mind, please keep me informed. I might be able to help you."

"Thank you. I will." With a smile, Tracie edged past the man. "I need to change for dinner. Thank you for helping out with our security and for letting us stay in your beautiful home."

He gave her a slight bow. "It is my pleasure."

Tracie hurried away. Feeling as if she were still being watched as she rounded a corner, she glanced back and saw Hector standing exactly where she'd left him, his gaze following her.

A shiver of apprehension coursed down her spine. Hank wouldn't warn her to trust no one without reason. Still, she felt guilty for deceiving Hector, when he'd opened up to her about his loss.

Back in the bedroom, Tracie avoided looking at the king-size bed where she and Rip would sleep that night. After the kiss they'd shared, she wasn't sure she could lie beside him and not want more.

Oh, hell. She knew she wouldn't be satisfied to just sleep with Rip. She wanted all of him, but was she willing to open her heart to a man? Especially a man who had heartache written into every muscle in his body? He was a SEAL. They'd never see each other and he'd be all over the world, possibly with a different woman in every port.

No. She couldn't risk her heart. Not so soon after her former fiancé had proven he was traitorous to the country she loved and had lied to her during their entire time together.

A little voice in her head reminded her that not all men were the same. Still, she wasn't ready to trust her instincts again. Not yet. Maybe never.

## Chapter Seven

Dinner was conducted in silence. Rip forced himself to eat, fueling his body for whatever was to come. Despite his resolve, the devil on his shoulder was pushing him to make love to Tracie before he had her full commitment to the possibility of a longer-term relationship.

He didn't know how long he could hold out and not take her to the next level, especially if they would be sleeping in the same room. For certain, he couldn't lie in the same bed and not touch her. It would be the floor for him. Hopefully, the discomfort would help to cool his desire.

As he sat at the long teak dining table that could have hosted a party of twenty, he stared across at Tracie.

She wore a simple black dress crisscrossed low in the front, exposing so much of her breasts, he couldn't look at her without his gaze drifting lower.

She'd twisted her silky brown hair up into some fancy knot at the back of her head, the long line of her throat tempting him nearly as much as the low-cut neckline of her dress. Several times he'd had to swallow hard to keep from groaning out loud.

When the meal was finally over, he nearly leaped to his feet. "I think I'll go for a walk."

Rising with more grace, Tracie raised her brows. "That sounds lovely. Do you mind if I join you?" Her lips quirked at the corners as if she knew he couldn't refuse her and knew he wanted to.

With the possibility that anyone could be watching, Rip nodded and held out his hand. "Please. I haven't had nearly as much time with my new bride as I'd like." He pulled her arm through his and guided her to the rear of the house and out through the patio door they'd gone through earlier.

The pool shone a soothing blue, the lights beneath the water tempting him. Later he'd come out on his own and swim a dozen laps to burn off some of the energy smoldering throughout his body. He wasn't used to taking things slow and he hadn't had an opportunity to work out since he'd met up with Tracie on this crazy mission Hank Derringer seemed to be in charge of.

Past the pool, several steps led down into a garden filled with every type of flower imaginable. Soft lights illuminated the path, pointing up to showcase one or another flowering bush or vine.

With Tracie so close, her bare arm touching his, Rip could almost imagine they really were on their honeymoon, enjoying a walk through a resort's grounds. When he reached a rose arbor, he stopped and turned her to face him, gathering her hands in his. "For the sake of our cover…"

Pulling her close, he circled her waist with one arm and cupped her chin with his free hand. Then he bent to kiss her.

Before his lips connected with hers, the rumble of an engine broke through the silence and darkness.

Tracie's body stiffened and they both turned their heads toward the sound.

It grew louder as an aircraft appeared, silhouetted against the moonlit sky.

"Think that might be our bodyguards?" Tracie asked, still standing in the circle of Rip's arm.

Rip returned his gaze to her face, her green eyes inky

dark and reflecting the light from the moon. "Right now, I really don't care. All I seem to be able to think about is kissing you."

Her gaze returned to his and she smiled. "Then what are you waiting for?"

"I haven't a clue." He captured the back of her head in his hand and kissed her, long and hard, his tongue pushing through to tangle with hers. When he finally came up for air, he leaned his forehead against hers. "What am I going to do with you?"

She brushed her thumb across his cheek and replied, "Make love—" Her words halted and she pressed her hand against his chest. "Never mind. Perhaps we should greet our bodyguards and fill them in on our plans."

"I wonder how much Hank told them?" Rip still wasn't sure about the Texas billionaire he had yet to meet.

"I suppose we'll find out." She led the way back to the house, walking a step ahead of Rip. He wanted to catch up to her and hold her arm like he had as they'd walked out to the garden, but he sensed she was putting distance between them on purpose.

As they entered the hacienda, Hector was descending the staircase. When he reached the bottom he met Rip and Tracie halfway across the wide foyer. "I believe Hank's men have arrived. My team are bringing them to the hacienda."

"Thank you." Rip moved up beside Tracie and slipped his arm around her waist. "I'd like to speak with them before we turn in for the night. Tomorrow will be a full and hopefully fruitful day."

"I've briefed my team on your needs. The man in charge speaks fluent English and will coordinate the details with your bodyguards once you decide on a plan. My men are prepared to ride out with you tomorrow as early as seven in the morning."

"Thank you, Hector." Rip held out his hand. "Your hospitality is exceptional."

Hector placed his hand in Rip's. "Say the word. I can do more."

"Thanks, but you've already done more than we could have hoped for."

With a nod to Rip and then Tracie, Hector backed toward the stairs. "If that is all you need of me, I will bid you *buenas noches*."

"Good night," Tracie echoed.

Rip merely nodded, his attention shifting to the hum of engines outside the front of the house.

He cupped Tracie's elbow and steered her toward the grand entrance.

A servant rushed forward and opened the heavy wooden door before Rip could reach out to open it for himself. He just couldn't get used to someone else doing things for him.

As when he and Tracie arrived, two Jeeps pulled up in front of the house, each mounted with machine guns. One had four of Hector's men on it with one manning the gun. The other Jeep had three of Hector's men and two additional men in the backseat.

As they climbed out of the back of the Jeep, they spoke in Spanish to the men in front. Both men had dark hair and swarthy skin and wore blue jeans and faded heather-gray T-shirts with no identifying marks on the fabric. With their appearance and nondescript clothing, they could easily have been any tourist or local.

The first one out walked up to Rip. "You must be Mr. Gideon. I'm Carlos Rodriguez, and my partner is Julio Jimenez. Mr. Derringer sent us to provide for your security while you're in Honduras. We can also translate for you if the need arises."

Rip nodded. "Call me Chuck."

Carlos nodded and repeated, "Chuck." He turned to Tracie. "Mrs. Gideon, it is a pleasure to meet you."

Tracie took the man's hand and shook it. "Please, I'm Phyllis. And it's nice to meet you, as well."

The men who'd brought them from the airplane jumped into the Jeeps and kicked up gravel as they spun out of the driveway and away to their posts, leaving the four of them alone.

Gripping Tracie's arm, Rip nodded toward the two men and said, "Let's walk."

Carlos fell in step with Rip on the opposite side of Tracie. "Hank said you might run into trouble with the guerillas who have taken over this area of Honduras. I'm not certain how much help the two of us will be against an entire army of them."

"Our host, Hector DeVita, has promised us the use of four of his men. Phyllis and I want to explore opportunities around the town of Colinas Rocosa. There is a plantation near there we want to pay a visit to, and Phyllis is interested in the town itself. If I'm not mistaken, there is a fiesta scheduled for tomorrow. Once we've concluded our business with the plantation owner, we'll join the festivities."

When they were far enough away from the house, Carlos stopped. "For the record, we're here to help a brother," he said and lifted his shirt aiming his tight abs toward the moonlight.

For a moment all Rip could see were dark spots across his skin. But as his gaze focused in on them he made out a tattoo of tiny frog footprints.

Rip smiled and relaxed. "I'm glad you're on board." He held out his hand. Carlos gripped his forearm and nodded solemnly then jerked his head toward Julio who also lifted his shirt and displayed another set of frog prints. Rip extended his arm to him, as well, and they clapped hands on each other's shoulders.

These men were SEALs. Whether they were on active duty or had since separated from the service. But once a SEAL, always a SEAL, and they stood by each other.

Knowing they had his six made him feel better about the mission. When they had a chance to get away from Hector's compound, he'd go into more detail with them. Having established that the men Hank had sent were just what he needed, Rip circled around and headed back toward the house.

"Did Hank send anymore information about the investigation?"

Carlos shook his head. "No. But he has Brandon working hard to find anything that will be of use to us."

"Good. Hector's men want to meet with us this evening to go over the timing of our travels tomorrow." Rip turned to Tracie. "I can fill you in on the details later, if you'd like to call it a night?"

Tracie chewed on her lower lip for a moment before nodding. "I'll leave you men to it. I am tired."

They'd arrived at the front of the hacienda and the steps leading up to the massive wooden front doors.

Rip walked Tracie up to the door and leaned down to touch his lips to hers. "I'll be up as soon as I nail down the details of our expedition tomorrow." He pressed his lips to the spot just below her earlobe and whispered, "I know you want to come with me."

"Yes, but you can handle this on your own. I really am tired."

Rip gazed into her eyes, his brows puckered. Finally, he opened the door for her and she disappeared inside.

He hadn't liked that she'd given in to him so easily. He'd find out what was eating her later, for now, he had work to do.

NORMALLY TRACIE WOULD have insisted on going with her partner to any planning sessions for the mission they would conduct. But after seeing the camaraderie of the SEAL men, she'd felt like an outsider. With Rip's kiss fresh on her lips and her emotions in a twist over everything that had happened that day, she needed the time alone.

She headed straight for their room and took the opportunity to prepare for bed without Rip making her feel incredibly hot and needy.

Hector's staff had been through the room and removed the dress they'd flung over the camera. Grabbing a lightweight throw blanket, she tossed it over the camera, not in the mood to be on display, now or ever.

Unfortunately, Hank's team had put together the perfect bridal trousseau and the only sleeping garment inside was now spread out across the sheets of the huge bed.

Tracie held up the scraps of material. The incredibly sexy, mostly sheer white teddy sported faux-fur trim around the lower-than-low neckline and where the elastic would stretch along her outer thighs.

How was she supposed to sleep in that? She riffled through drawers of clothing the staff had unpacked from her suitcases and found one dark, long-sleeved T-shirt and a pair of dark jeans, apparently for any night ops they might need to conduct.

Well, it was nighttime and she wasn't sleeping in the faux-fur bit of fluff. Not when Rip would be lying in the bed beside her.

Not only would it tickle her, but every time she moved,

she'd be reminded of how close Rip was and how far he'd pushed away from her since the shower.

The teddy was definitely out. She wadded it into a tight ball and shoved it under the pillow, stripped out of her clothes and pulled the T-shirt over her head. It fit her perfectly. Therein lay the problem. It wasn't long enough to cover her bottom. Her pulse pounding, not knowing when Rip would be back in the room, Tracie slipped beneath the sheets and pulled them up over her. The long-sleeved black T-shirt stood out against the crisp white sheets.

A knock on the door made her jump. "Who is it?" she responded, remembering she hadn't locked the door, leaving the lock open for when Rip returned.

"*Pardon, Señora.* It is Dehlia Perez. I have fresh towels for your bath."

"Just a minute." Knowing how strange she must look in the black T-shirt, Tracie shucked it, grabbed the white teddy and pulled it over her head, tugging it down over her torso. Shoving the black T-shirt beneath the sheet by her feet, she leaned back against the pillow and pulled the sheet up over her breasts. "Okay, you can come in now."

The door opened and the maid entered, wearing the powder-blue uniform and carrying a stack of clean, thick white towels. She closed the door behind her and hurried toward the bathroom. When she came back out, she walked directly over to Tracie.

"*Bueno?*"

"Yes." Tracie smiled at the woman and willed her to leave so that she could change back into the black T-shirt before Rip returned. "*Gracias.*"

Slowly, the woman walked backward, her gaze skimming through the room, looking for anything out of place or needing attention. Her glance shifted to the blanket hanging from the light fixture, but she didn't say anything. She reached the door and opened it. *"Buenos noches, Señora."*

"Good night." Tracie let go of the breath she'd been holding and listened for the sound of footsteps retreating down the hallway before she reached for the snaps between her legs.

No sooner had her hands dived beneath the sheets, the door opened and Rip stepped in.

Tracie froze as Rip's gaze swept across the faux fur barely covering her nipples.

His nostrils flared as his fingers twisted the lock on the door.

Based on his instant response, Tracie knew the man was interested. Though she wished he'd quit giving her mixed signals.

Too late to trade the teddy for the T-shirt, she pulled the sheet up over the faux fur and the rounded swells of her breasts.

"Woman, you don't know what you're doing to me," Rip grumbled, low and barely audible.

Nevertheless, Tracie heard him. Her back straightened and she sat up, letting the sheet fall down around her waist. The teddy was so sheer it didn't hide much beneath the soft white fabric.

"Sweetheart, you had your chance and blew it." Yanking the comforter off the end of the bed, she threw it at him and followed that with a pillow that hit him in the side of his head. "You can sleep on the floor."

She plopped back against the pillow and waited, her breath lodged in her throat. Half of her hoped he'd accept the challenge and crawl into bed with her, while the other half wished he'd just leave her alone. She was tired of the push-me-pull-me game he had been playing.

Rip caught the blanket, his lips thinning. He didn't say a word as he settled on the floor at the foot of the bed.

So that was how he was going to play it?

Tracie turned her back on the man, punched her pillow, wishing it was him, and settled in for a restless night's sleep.

Tomorrow promised to be a long day. With Rip at her side, it would prove more difficult than it had to be.

## Chapter Eight

Rip didn't know how long he lay staring up at the ceiling before he fell into a fitful doze. He'd slept on worse than the hard floor beneath him. One time he'd slept in a fox-hole filled with cold water. By the time he'd gotten out of it, he thought for sure he'd sprouted webs between his toes.

Sure the hardwood floors were unforgiving on his back, but the discomfort came solely from the image seared into his mind of Tracie lying against the pillows in that…that… *holy hell.*

That teddy had him tied in knots. He could imagine tasting the rounded swells of her breasts all the way to the edge of the faux fur that would tickle his nose and force him to strip the garment from her body. Then where would they be?

She'd be nude and he'd forget the reason he couldn't allow himself to sleep with her. He slammed a fist into the pillow and turned on his side, the floor biting into his hipbone and shoulder. *Damn it to hell.* The woman was derailing him when he needed to be thinking solely about the mission.

As the gray light of predawn pushed through the blinds on the windows, Rip rose from the hardwood floor, tilt-ing his head from side to side to work the kinks out of his neck. He draped the blanket and pillow on the end of the bed, careful not to disturb Tracie, and he entered the bathroom where he took a long cold shower before donning his disguise of the wealthy young entrepreneur.

The suit he chose was a lightweight gray linen but it was still a suit. He skipped the tie and opted for a black polo shirt. He'd carry the jacket and only wear it when he met with the plantation owner. As hot as it got in Honduras, he didn't want to wear any more clothes than he had to.

When he emerged from the shower, Tracie still lay in the bed her eyes closed.

His gaze lingered on her face. Her dark hair splayed out in a fan across the white pillowcase. If he was not mistaken, her eyelid jerked and lifted halfway before closing tightly.

He strode across the floor and swatted her hip. "You're not fooling me. You might as well get up."

She opened her eyes, rolled onto her back and stretched her arms over her head. The movement edged the sheet down below her chest, making the faux fur of the teddy rise as her back arched.

Rip spun on his heels and marched toward the door. "I'll see you at the breakfast table."

Her warm chuckle halted him as he reached for the door.

"Not a morning person, I take it?" she said.

Yes, he was a morning person. But he wanted to do more than just say good morning. She'd made it clear he'd missed his chance, and he wasn't willing to go back on his word, anyway. "We leave in forty-five minutes," he said through clenched teeth and left the room.

Leaving Tracie in that sheer white teddy was harder to do than to storming an enemy position in the middle of a firefight. Every ounce of his being wanted to go right back into the bedroom and show her what lovemaking was all about. Whoever she'd been engaged to before had been a first-class idiot.

After their initial meeting, Rip knew that Tracie was a woman worth fighting for—it was worth taking it slowly and bringing her up to a point where she would be willing to commit to the possibility of a future. She wasn't a one-night stand kind of woman.

*"Buenos dias, Señor Gideon."* Hector sat at the dining table, buttering a soft tortilla. He pointed to the seat across from him. "Have a seat. My staff will get whatever you'd like to eat for breakfast."

"I'd like coffee. Straight up, black, no cream or sugar."

Hector nodded to a servant who hurried from the room and returned with a mug of steaming brew. The scent of freshly ground coffee cleared the cobwebs from Rip's mind and made a good start to getting him back on track.

Hector set his fork beside his plate and crossed his arms. "Senor Gideon, you strike me as someone who has been a member of the military."

"My father was in the US Marine Corp," he said, avoiding a direct lie.

"Did you follow your father's lead and enter the military?"

Rip was in midsip of his coffee and took the time to phrase his answer, wondering how he could respond without giving anything away.

He was saved by the appearance of one of Hector's male servants who entered the room and spoke in rapid-fire Spanish. Rip could only catch a few of his words.

Hector's eyes narrowed and his brow inched downward as the man spoke.

The lead guard who'd met Rip at the airplane entered, his boots clomping across the smooth tile floor, a deep scowl across his forehead.

Hector glared at the man and pushed to his feet. "Pardon

me, Senor Gideon. It seems we have had a breach in our security that I must deal with."

"By all means. Security of your home takes priority." Rip half stood and dropped back into his seat as Hector moved into the hallway and exchanged harsh words with the guard.

Rip understood Spanish and got by all right speaking it, but he was by no means fluent. Still, he picked up enough of Hector's conversation to get the gist of what had happened.

A truck had crashed into the concrete outer wall. Though it was full of explosive fertilizer, by some gift of fate it had not ignited. However, it had ripped a hole in the concrete that would need to be repaired. Until the repairs were complete, a guard would have to be posted at that point, as well.

Hector wanted to know who was responsible. Who had set the truck in motion to crash into his wall? And when he found that person, he wanted him brought to the compound where he would be made an example of.

Out of the corner of his eye, Rip witnessed his congenial host go from a well-mannered, soft-spoken and civilized man to the steel-edged commander of his little corner of the Honduras countryside.

If Rip was certain he could trust the man, he'd want him on his side not against him. When he finished breakfast, he didn't wait around, preferring to allow Tracie to eat on her own rather than face her after the lousy night's sleep he'd had.

As he left the dining room, Tracie descended the staircase.

Rip stood in the shadows of the dining room until she reached the bottom, enjoying the view. She wore a silky sundress in a soft butter yellow with narrow straps and a hip-hugging skirt. Low, matching heels showed off her trim ankles and well-toned calves. Her hair hung down around her shoulders and she carried a broad-brimmed hat with a sky-blue scarf tied to it.

Rip stepped through the door. "I trust you slept well, Mrs. Gideon?" He greeted her with a quick kiss on her lips.

Tracie's eyes widened at first and then her lips pushed up in a smile. "I did, Mr. Gideon."

He suspected she was lying, playing the part. Makeup barely disguised the dark circles beneath her eyes.

"I'll see to the vehicles for our excursion while you find something to eat."

"I'm ready to go."

"Please, find something to eat. Things don't always go as planned and, for all we know, you might not get another meal today."

Tracie's fists knotted and she stared into his eyes. "You think things will go that bad?"

"A number of scenarios could take place. It's best to go into a fight with fuel in your belly."

"Fine. I'll find something to eat."

"And I'll be outside mustering the troops." He chucked her beneath the chin like a kid sister to keep from yanking her into his arms and crushing her with a kiss. "Now go. If you're not outside in fifteen minutes, I'll leave you here."

"Like hell you will." She spun on her pretty heels and hurried from the foyer, headed toward the dining room.

He liked her spunk but worried about her running in heels. Hopefully, they wouldn't be running today. They'd do their recon and save the running and covert ops for the cover of darkness.

Tracie bypassed the dining room, unwilling to wait for an order to be created and delivered and found her way to the hacienda's spacious, modern kitchen where she used her tenuous grasp on Spanish to ask for a piece of toast and a slice from a ham sitting in a roasting pan on top of the counter. She folded the ham into the toast, wrapped it in napkin, grabbed a cup of freshly squeezed orange juice and hurried outside.

She'd be damned if Rip left her behind now that the two SEALs had arrived. Hank had assigned her to this case. She was Rip's covert bride. They'd established the newly-wed cover story, they had to see it through—SEALs or no SEALs. And she was every bit as qualified to go on this mission as they were.

When she arrived outside in her feminine sundress to find Hector's bodyguards dressed in camouflage uniforms and packing M4A1s, she almost turned around and ran back inside to change into slacks and combat boots.

"There you are." Rip hooked her arm to keep her from changing her clothes. "You look so pretty today, I'm afraid I'll be beating the locals off with a stick."

Falling into his story line, she smiled up at him. "I wanted to wear something nice. If we're going to the fiesta in Colinas Rocosa, I wanted to be dressed for dancing."

"Hopefully our business arrangements won't take all day and we can enjoy the festivities."

The two SEALs joined them dressed in jeans and loose-fitting guayabera shirts. When the wind picked up a little, the shirts pressed against their bellies, outlining suspicious lumps Tracie suspected were the pistols they had strapped beneath their clothing. From all outward appearances, they would blend into a festival crowd with their dark brown hair, bronze skin and fluent Spanish.

On one hand, Tracie was uneasy about Hector's para-military bodyguards following them on the trip. They could be a big fat sign to the guerillas that the people they were guarding might make good kidnapping targets. On the other hand, they looked big, bad and dangerous and might just scare off any unwanted attempts to steal the wealthy play-boy and his bride to hold them for ransom.

Having been kidnapped once, Tracie had no desire to go through that again. She'd been lucky to get out alive. In cat terminology, she'd already used up one of her spare lives. Why tempt fate and use up another?

"Having second thoughts?" Rip whispered as he helped her into her seat in the Jeep. He tucked her skirt around her legs, his big fingers sending electrical shocks up her thighs and to her core as they brushed her skin through the thin fabric of her dress.

Tracie had been around plenty of testosterone-fueled men, having gone through Quantico where women made up less than 20 percent of the trainees. But Rip was some-how more masculine and more dangerous than any man she'd ever known.

She responded with, "No second thoughts about the plan for the day." Definitely second thoughts about the SEAL tucking her into the backseat of the Jeep. She could imag-ine those gentle hands sliding over her naked skin, stirring up so much passion she'd be lost, maybe even forget her vow to never trust a man again.

Julio slid in behind the steering wheel, Carlos rode shot-gun, his hand resting lightly over the weapon beneath his shirt.

As Rip settled into the seat beside her, Tracie's pulse leaped. This was it. Up until this point, they'd been in a fairly safe environment having flown into a private airstrip to be met by armed guards and secluded behind a massive concrete and concertina-wire wall.

She sucked in a deep breath as they drove through heavy gates onto the public road. Rip gathered her hand in his and rested it on his thigh. The gesture made her pulse slow from its frantic beating. It also made her realize how much she'd grown to trust this SEAL in the very short time they'd been together, giving her the confidence to see this mission through. She hadn't realized how affected she'd been by her previous captivity at the hands of Mexican thugs.

Mexico had been much like Honduras. With drug cartels in charge of the country, whoever had the most or the biggest guns were in charge.

In Honduras the guerillas called the shots, undermining and manipulating the government.

Using GPS, Julio sped along the road slowing only for the occasional cattle or goats being herded by small, skinny children or teens. Nothing about the lush green countryside raised red flags. They could have been traveling tourists without a care in the world. Except they were in a guerilla-infested area of Honduras.

As they passed through Colinas Rocosa, Tracie made note of the town. Decorated with crepe-paper streamers, and a sign commemorating the town's patron saint, who they were celebrating, the streets were filled with vendors selling their wares. Most folks smiled and waved, happy to have something to rejoice—grasping at a chance to have fun in a land where danger lurked around every corner.

Tracie found herself peering into every vehicle they passed on the road, wondering if the occupants were part of the guerilla faction.

One particular truck sped toward them moving too fast for the narrow, people-filled streets.

A small child darted out into the middle of the road, directly into the path of the oncoming vehicle.

"Stop!" Tracie shouted.

Julio slammed on the brakes and the Jeep skidded to a halt.

Tracie leaped from the vehicle, snatched the boy from the

middle of the road and stepped back as the truck barreled by, its driver barely glancing her way.

The boy clung to her and burst into tears.

Tracie held him against her breast, rubbing his back and whispering soothing words as she did so. A moment later, a woman's wail broke through the child's sobs and his mother ran out into the street, her eyes wide.

As soon as the boy heard his mother's voice, he struggled to break free Tracie's hold. She set him on the ground and he ran into his mother's arms, crying even louder.

The frightened mother scooped up her errant youngster and hugged him hard to her chest. *"Gracias, Señora. Muchas gracias."* Then bowing and apologizing in Spanish, she hurried away, talking sternly to her little one.

A hand slipped around Tracie's waist and Rip pulled her against him. "That was close."

"Too close." Tracie leaned into Rip's embrace for a moment, willing her pulse to slow to normal. Then she glanced up at him. "That truck driver didn't even slow down."

"No, he didn't. For a moment there, I thought he'd hit you." His hand shook where it rested on her waist. "I admit I've never been more scared."

She stared up at him. "You? Scared?"

"Hey, just because I'm a S— man…doesn't mean I can't get scared." He hugged her hard, then bent to kiss her. A sharp, high-pitched beep made Tracy look around.

A man on a vintage motorcycle passed on the street, grinning.

Her cheeks heating, Tracie realized they were the center of attention with the two SEALs in the front seat of the Jeep, Hector's men in the vehicle behind and the citizens of Colinas Rocosa gathering around them.

A woman walked by and patted Tracie on the back saying something in rapid Spanish she couldn't quite translate.

"What did she say?" Tracie asked.

"Something about young love and having babies of your own."

Her face heating even more, Tracie forced a snort. "Like that's going to happen. Not in my line of work." Her voice was low enough only Rip could hear her.

"It can happen," Rip reassured her.

"Not today." Stepping out of Rip's embrace, Tracie couldn't help the feeling of loss that washed over her. She'd just have to get over it. Their days together were numbered and babies with Rip were completely out of the question.

Then why did a dark-haired, blue-eyed little girl emerge in her mind, holding hands with her and Rip and swinging between them?

Tracie climbed back into the Jeep and tucked her own skirts around her before Rip had the chance. Her thoughts were unsettling. She liked working for Hank and wouldn't want to give up what she did to go all domestic.

Still…that little boy had felt good and somehow right in her arms.

What was she thinking? Her life didn't have room for a husband and children.

But if it did…Rip was the kind of man she'd want to marry. Too bad her job pretty much ensured she would die single.

## Chapter Nine

The trip to the plantation went without a hitch. Too easy. Rip's every nerve was on alert.

As they turned onto the gravel road leading to the main house, a man with an automatic weapon stepped out of the shadows of the overhanging trees into the middle of the road aiming the weapon at the driver.

*Ah, there it was. The threat.*

To Rip, it was almost a relief to finally see the enemy.

The man shouted in Spanish for them to stop.

Julio immediately applied the brakes, jamming his foot on the pedal so hard, Rip and Tracie were thrown forward.

The Jeep behind them slid to a stop mere inches from their bumper and the men aboard leaped to the ground, aiming their guns at the man in the middle of the road.

Rip got out of the Jeep, smiling and holding his hands in the air. "Let's not get crazy here."

Carlos translated to the man in the middle of the road.

He answered back, talking so fast, Rip couldn't understand him.

Five more men emerged from the shadows, all bearing arms.

Rip's chest tightened, but he held his ground. "Tell them that we are here to see the owner of the plantation, that we mean no harm."

Carlos translated.

The guard in charge snarled and jerked his head toward Hector's men.

"He wants your men to put down their weapons."

"Tell him they will when he confirms he works for the plantation owner." Rip gritted his teeth.

Before he could stop her, Tracie stepped out of the vehicle and came around to his side. He wished like hell she'd stayed put in the vehicle.

Instead, she stood beside him in her yellow sundress and curled her arm through his, looking like a ray of sunshine, all soft and feminine, with nerves of steel hidden beneath that pretty dress. "What seems to be the problem, sweetheart?"

Reminding himself that he wasn't armed for combat and others' lives depended on him keeping a cool head, Rip patted her hand. "Nothing but a little misunderstanding."

Carlos spoke in Spanish to the head guard again.

The man pulled a walkie-talkie from a case on his belt and barked into it.

A moment later a voice crackled from the device.

Carlos turned to Rip. "Delgado just gave the go-ahead to let us through as long as we leave Hector's men and all our weapons behind."

"Okay, then." Rip nodded to Carlos.

Carlos and Julio tossed their weapons on the ground and held their hands in the air while the guards patted them down. Then Carlos gave instructions to Hector's men.

They didn't look happy about being left out of the action, but they backed away, still holding their weapons at the ready.

Rip smiled at the plantation gate guards. "Then we're good?"

The guards stepped back, forming a line on either side

of the road with the man in charge climbing aboard a dusty old forty-horsepower motorcycle the likes of which hadn't been built since the end of World War II.

It belched smoke and kicked up dust that streamed through the open doors and windows of the Jeeps, forcing Julio to hang back to let the dust settle before they followed.

The road curved through a hedge of encroaching jungle. On one side of the lane, in the rare gaps between trees, vines and underbrush, Rip could see the coffee orchards spread out over the hills and valleys, lush and green. On the opposite side of the road, the jungle seemed impenetrable and free of the coffee trees that produced the heavenly brew.

The next curve revealed a wide opening in the jungle where a traditional plantation-style house rose up from the surrounding orchard and jungle, the base a dull gray stone with a multitude of arched passages. The stark white of the upper story lay in bright contrast to the surrounding deep green vegetation.

The guard on the motorcycle in front of them parked the vehicle and ducked through one of the arches.

Julio brought the Jeep to a smooth stop. Rip was first out.

The guard emerged again with another man dressed in jeans, a white button-up shirt, black vest and a cowboy hat. On his hips rode a gun holster just like those seen in the Old West. If Rip wasn't mistaken, the gun in the holster was a vintage Colt single-action US Army revolver with a pearl handle, in mint condition. His face was that of the scarred man in the photos Morris Franks had stashed in his car.

"Nice gun you've got there." Rip held out his hand. "Name's Chuck Gideon. This is my wife, Phyllis. We stopped by to talk to the owner of *le Plantación de Ángel*."

The man rested his hand on the pearl grip and in heavily accented English responded. "I, Carmelo Delgado, am the owner of *le Plantación de Ángel*. What do you want?"

Rip curled his arm around Tracie's waist and smiled. "My wife fancies owning a coffee plantation, and she fell in love with the name of this one. Have you considered selling?"

The man's heavy brows V'd toward the bridge of his nose. "No." He turned to go back into the house.

Rip stepped forward. "Surely there is a price we could agree on. Phyllis has her heart set on growing her own coffee."

Delgado shot his riposte over his shoulder. "Then buy another farm. This one is not for sale."

When the man started toward the house, Rip stepped in front of him, blocking his return to the cooler interior.

No sooner had Rip moved, than half a dozen armed men stepped out of the shadows on the other sides of the arches. Each carried a M4A1 rifle, exactly like the ones used by the US Army. Rip used a specially modified version. The ones pointing at him now were pristine and new.

Rip raised his hands. "Hey, hey. No need to get punchy. I'm a businessman not much into playing with guns. I prefer to concentrate my efforts on making money." He addressed Delgado. "Could we talk?" Glancing sideways at the men with the guns, he added, "In private. I might have a deal you'll be interested in."

The man glared down his nose at Rip. "I do not think so."

Rip's smile slipped and his brows descended, all joviality wiped from his expression as he examined the guns the men carried. "I take it you like the weapons your men carry." He nodded toward the closest one. "What would you say if I told you that I could get them for you at a cheaper price?"

Tracie stiffened next to him, but her expression remained the same. The woman could probably play a mean hand of poker.

Delgado's eyes narrowed and he stared from Rip to Tracie and back to Rip. "I'd say for you to get the hell off my land."

Rip shrugged. "Have it your way. If you want to keep buying guns at a higher price, that's your business. We will be on our way." Rip turned toward the Jeep.

Tracie turned with him.

The hired guns blocked their exit.

Rip's muscles bunched, prepared to fight his way out if necessary.

The plantation owner jerked his head and gave an order in Spanish.

The guards stepped back, giving Rip and Tracie an open path to escape.

Delgado sliced the air with his hand. "Now go. You are not welcome here."

"Your loss," Rip said. "You could have sold the plantation and purchased some damned fine weapons at a steal of a price. Come on, sweetheart, at least we can enjoy the festival tonight." Rip shook his head, hooked Tracie's elbow in his hand and guided her to the backseat of the Jeep.

Once they were all in, Julio spun the vehicle around and headed back the way they'd entered.

When they were out of earshot, Tracie leaned close to Rip and demanded, "What in the hell was that all about?"

Rip leaned back in his seat, a grin spreading across his lips. "I think we hit the jackpot."

"Meaning?" she shot back.

"Meaning, I went to the plantation hoping to look around the land for hideouts, thinking maybe the guerilla group is camping out on the grounds. Instead, I think we found some of them."

Tracie nodded. "I get that. They carried the guns from

the DEA agent's photographs. But why did you tell them we had guns to sell?"

"The offer to purchase the plantation wasn't enough. The temptation of cheaper weapons? Now that got his attention. And I was beginning to think he wasn't going to let us leave so easily."

TRACIE INHALED DEEPLY and let it out. "Wow. We've gone from being just a couple on our honeymoon looking for a coffee plantation, to international arms dealers. It's insanely dangerous." She gave a shaky smile. "But what the hell. I'm in."

Rip clapped his hands together. "We have a festival to go to, and I'll bet money that, one, Delgado has something to do with the guerillas since he has access to the weapons we're looking for. And two, he'll have us tailed. All we have to do is identify his men at the festival, plant tracking devices on one or two of them and see where they lead." He grinned. "You ready for a late-night adventure?"

Her heartbeat kicked up when he smiled at her like that, and adrenaline ran through her veins, making her wish they were already following the tracking devices to the guerrilla's hidden location deep in the jungle. "I'm ready."

As they passed the entrance to the plantation, they picked up Hector's vehicle full of mercenaries.

Tracie hadn't liked the mean look in Delgado's eyes. Several times, she'd glanced back over her shoulder, trying to look past Hector's men to the road beyond. A couple of times the road straightened long enough she thought she saw another vehicle kicking up dust.

Within twenty minutes, they were back in Colinas Rocosa, driving slowly through the busy streets.

"Are we stopping here?" Carlos asked.

"No," Rip responded. "We'll come back later this evening. We can go back to Hector's and enjoy the pool during the hottest part of the day."

Tracie touched his arm. "We can't go back to Hector's. Carmelo's men could be following us."

Rip grinned. "We'll take care of that." He leaned forward. "Julio, when we get to the outskirts of Colinas Rocosa pull over."

"Aye, aye!" Julio said and pulled over a moment later.

"Carlos," Rip said. "Could you please explain to Hector's men that they can return to his place? We no longer require their services."

Carlo's brows rose. "If you're sure we can handle it just the four of us."

"Julio assures me he's an expert driver. I'm counting on that to throw Carmelo's men off our trail before we head back to Hector's."

*"Muy bueno."* When the other Jeep slid to a stop behind them, Carlos met the leader of the group and spoke softly in Spanish. The man nodded and barked an order to the driver. The Jeep left them, headed back to Hector's.

Carlos climbed back into their vehicle. "I told them to take a roundabout route back. But they should get there before us."

"Good, now let's lose our tail." Rip patted Julio's shoulder. "Go."

Tracie glanced back toward the little town and spotted a truck filled with what looked like Delgado's men moving slowly toward them.

Julio slammed his foot on the accelerator. Dust and gravel spewed out behind them as they shot forward.

Tracie held on to the armrest, her hair flying around her face. A rush of excitement filled her as Julio sped away from Delgado's men.

The road twisted and turned through the hills and Tracie

lost sight of the truck for a second. The next turn she spotted it. They were falling behind, but not by enough to lose them.

Ahead the road T-junctioned.

Julio turned to the right, stirring up a lot of dust and then spun around and rolled more slowly back the opposite direction.

Tracie swiveled in her seat to see the road behind her. They'd lost time turning around and going back the other direction.

A curve in the road meant the jungle blocked her view of the intersection.

Abruptly, the Jeep left the road and plowed into the underbrush. Giant trees shaded the spot where they'd entered the jungle, hopefully hiding their entry point.

Julio shut off the engine and jumped out of the Jeep, followed by Carlos and Rip. Together, they pushed and shoved brush and vines over the branches broken by their plunge into the woods. When they were satisfied with their efforts, they stood still.

Dressed in heels, Tracie remained where she was, listening as the sounds of nature resumed, disturbed only by the rumbling of tires on gravel and the heavy roar of a truck's engine.

Rip crossed to Tracie and whispered, "They turned right at the intersection."

She nodded, afraid to speak too loud, even though the men in the truck probably couldn't hear them.

The truck's engine sounds faded the farther away they moved from the team hidden in the vegetation.

"Sounds like they're gone," Tracie said.

Rip held up a hand. "We need to be certain."

Carlos closed the distance between them. "I'm going on recon."

Rip nodded.

Slipping into the jungle, Carlos hunched low, moving so quietly Tracie couldn't hear his footsteps. A moment later he disappeared.

Tracie leaned close to Rip and whispered into his ear, "How long should we wait to be certain?"

Rip's lips hovered next to her temple. "Until Carlos returns." His breath stirred the loose tendrils of hair around her ear, sending ripples of awareness across her skin. A thin sheen of sweat built up across her upper lip that had nothing to do with the heat and humidity of the jungle.

Just when Tracie had relaxed and thought they were in the clear, the sound of an engine approaching made her stiffen. "Delgado's men or someone else?" she said, speaking quietly.

The engine noise grew louder and then seemed to hold steady for a moment. Shouts pierced the air. Too far away to make out what was being said, Tracie sent up a silent prayer that Carlos was all right and hadn't been discovered.

The engine's rumble changed and then started to fade again. A few minutes later, Carlos emerged from the darkness of the surrounding jungle.

"They're gone."

"What happened?"

Carlos's lips twisted. "They'd left a couple of soldiers at the intersection. I was only three feet away from one of them before I saw him."

"Damn." Rip grinned. "I take it you saw him, but he didn't see you?"

Carlos gave Rip an answering grin. "Damn right. I lay low, waiting for him to move far enough away I could slip back to you and let you know. But it wasn't until the truck returned that he left his post. Their leader was angry that they'd lost us and mentioned that Delgado wouldn't be happy. They loaded the two guards and headed back to Colinas Rocosa."

"Good." Rip climbed into the Jeep. "We can go back to Hector's now. I hope the others made it back without being followed."

Tracie was glad to see the imposing concrete fence and concertina wire rise up out of the jungle when they arrived at Hector's. She'd be even happier when she got out of the dress and heels. Never had she felt so useless. When they returned to the festival, she planned on wearing a dress, but she'd have serviceable shoes and trousers beneath the skirt.

Having grown up on a ranch, dresses made her itch to be back in her jeans. The FBI had suited her perfectly. She dressed to suit the mission. Usually that was in trousers. This undercover bride stuff was challenging her inner tomboy to the limits.

Though she had to admit, the look in Rip's eye when he'd first seen her in the yellow sundress almost made it worth the discomfort.

This evening the real test would be following the guerillas back to their jungle hideout. If all went as planned, they'd get the information they sought and be on their way back to the States tomorrow.

## Chapter Ten

As they pulled in front of the sprawling hacienda, Hector emerged from the house, his brow puckered. "*Mi amigos.* I worried when you did not return with my men."

Rip climbed out of the Jeep and met the man at the base of the steps. "The owner of *le Plantación de Ángel* seemed to want to follow us back to our place of origin. I didn't think you wanted them to know I was staying here, so we led them on what we call a wild goose chase." He grinned. "It was entertaining to say the least."

Hector's gaze shifted to Tracie. "And you, Senora? Were you equally entertained?" he asked, his tone doubtful.

Tracie slipped her hand into the crook of Rip's elbow. "Very much so. I felt like I was on the set of an action-adventure movie. It was exhilarating." She smiled and shook her hair back from her face.

The motion made Rip's pulse quicken. How he'd love to run his hands through her pretty brown hair. She'd been stoic and held it together throughout the entire confrontation with Delgado.

Their host's frown deepened. "Carmelo Delgado is not a man to be toyed with. He will not be happy that he couldn't find you. Were you able to speak to him about buying a coffee plantation?"

Rip pressed his lips together, aiming for a sufficient look of irritation. "He didn't want to sell his place."

Tracie touched his arm. "Oh, honey, he was quite adamant. He even had his people point guns at us." She raised a hand to her breast, although Rip was certain she didn't have to feign her shock at their hostile reception on *le Plantación de Ángel*. She dropped her hand and looked around. "I don't know about you, but all that excitement made me hungry."

Hector hesitated, his eyes narrowing as if he wasn't convinced they were telling him everything. Then his brows rose and he waved toward the door. "Please. I will have my staff prepare a meal."

"And I so look forward to swimming in that lovely pool," Tracie said.

Rip could have kissed her for pulling Hector's attention off their day's adventure and back to his duties as a host. His gut told him that Hector was on the up-and-up and could be trusted with the truth, but Rip wasn't going to risk the lives of Tracie, Carlos and Julio on instinct. They entered the hacienda and settled down to a meal in the airy dining room. Afterward, Tracie excused herself and left the men to talk, claiming a headache.

Hector received a call at the end of the meal and left the room to go to his office to take it.

Rip stood and motioned to Carlos and Julio. "Please, let's go out to the pool to discuss tonight's plan. My wife wishes to attend the festival, but I worry that Delgado's men will be there. I want to make certain we have a way out, should things get sticky."

Carlos's gaze shifted left then right before he nodded. "Let's go."

Once outside, Rip settled in chairs far enough away from the hacienda walls they need not worry about listening devices. Carlos and Julio dragged seats close to him and they put their heads together. The night ahead could prove to be difficult.

"It might be suicide going to the festival tonight," Carlos started.

Rip nodded. He wasn't sure he liked the idea himself. "I'll check in with Hank before we go. If they haven't been able to locate the rebel base, we have to get close enough to Delgado's men to plant GPS devices on them."

"If they attend."

"They will." Rip grinned. "I told them we'd be there."

Carlos's mouth quirked up on the corner. "You did, didn't you?"

"Purposely," Rip said. "And with the suggestion I was a competing weapons supplier, I don't think he will try to kidnap us. Follow, yes. Kidnap or kill, no."

Carlos frowned. "From Hank's briefing, these guerillas prefer to shoot first, question later."

"We'll be prepared."

Julio leaned close. "Hank sent along enough equipment to outfit an entire SEAL team. All we need is for Delgado's team to lead us into their camp."

"Good. Let's be sure to take what we need with us. I have a feeling we'll be headed into the jungle before the night is over."

"What will you tell Hector?" Carlos asked.

"Leave it to me."

Julio's eyes narrowed. "He'll want to send reinforcements with us. I prefer to leave them behind. We can handle this mission without them."

"They might prove a good distraction. Delgado won't know who to target if he has eight people to follow instead of just the four of us. I'll have Hector instruct them to dress casual like they're going to the festival and leave the big guns at the house."

Julio laughed. "Yeah, the camouflage might give them away."

Carlos nodded. "We'll have to lose them, as well, or risk them following us to the rebel camp."

Rip stared at the two men and felt a kinship, even though they'd only met the night before. "What unit were you with?"

"SEAL Team Six," Julio answered.

"And you're working for Hank now?"

Julio nodded. "He recruited us when he'd heard we'd left the Navy."

"Why'd you leave?" Rip asked.

"Our missions were becoming too bogged down in politics," Carlos answered.

"Yeah. Watched one of our own get gunned down because we weren't allowed to fire first."

Rip sucked in a deep breath. "I understand that. We're here because someone in our government ratted out the DEA agent we went in to rescue. Set us up to pull him out far enough for a sniper to take him down and we lost one of our team."

Carlos and Julio nodded.

"That's what Hank told us." Carlos's mouth pressed into a tight line. "Makes you wonder who you're fighting for."

Julio's brows dipped. "When we heard about your situation, we asked to be a part of the team."

Rip's chest tightened. "I'm glad you're on board." A movement out of the corner of his eye caught his attention.

Tracie, emerged from the hacienda wearing a hot-pink bikini and a sheer wrap knotted around her hips. The ends of the wrap billowed out in the breeze and then plastered against her shapely legs.

Carlos gave a low whistle. "None of our buddies looked like that in the Navy."

"Yeah," Julio said. "Glad she's on our team."

Rip's fists clenched. He wanted to tell the guys to back off, but what good would it do? Tracie had been clear about not wanting a relationship with him. On this four-person team, Rip was the outsider. Julio, Carlos and Tracie worked for Hank.

"Hank said she was a Fed," Carlos said.

"Former FBI," Rip confirmed. "I would have thought you three would know each other."

Carlos shook his head. "Julio and I are out of San Diego. We've only been to Hank's ranch once. When he has a job, he either picks up the phone or takes one of his planes and meets with us in California."

"Just how many people does Hank have working for him?"

Julio shrugged. "None of us know. He started with four cowboys from Texas. Since then, he's expanded out. I think he has one in Colorado, the two of us in California and now a woman. All of us were born and raised on ranches."

Which would exclude Rip from Hank's selection criteria. He'd never been on a ranch in his life, having grown up in the suburbs of Atlanta, raised by his father, a member of the Atlanta Police Department. Not that he cared about Hank's methods of choosing his Covert Cowboys. He wasn't interested in giving up on the Navy SEALs yet. He loved his job, despite the corruption within the government.

If he could trace the source of the weapons sales back to the United States, he was almost certain he'd find a corrupt government official at the root of the problem. Clean out the traitor and he could go back to business as usual.

Silence fell over the three men as they sat in the shade, studying Tracie as she strode out into the sunshine, untied the wrap and let it fall onto a lounge chair.

Her body was trim, not an ounce of flab, her muscles

tight and well defined. She'd let her hair hang straight down her back. Her skin was tanned, not too dark, but a perfect contrast to the bright pink of the bikini. For a moment she stood at the edge of the pool, staring across the hilltop to the east, as if she could see all the way to the coast.

Rip's breath caught in his throat. She was as beautiful in the bikini as she'd been naked in the shower and he wanted her even more. What would it take to break through her defenses and convince her they had a chance?

Then she sucked in a deep breath, her lungs expanding before she dove cleanly into the sparkling water.

When she surfaced, Carlos and Julio clapped loudly and whistled.

"Well done, Senora Gideon," Carlos said.

Tracie twisted in the water, pushing the wet hair back from her forehead. "I didn't see y'all there," she said in her soft Texas drawl. "Am I missing anything?"

Rip shook his head. "Not really. We were discussing going to the festival tonight."

"Oh, good. I haven't danced since our wedding." She winked at Rip.

"Ah, the beautiful Senora Gideon is taking advantage of the pool." Hector stepped out of the shadows, wearing swim trunks with a towel slung around his neck. "The pool sees so little use with only me to enjoy its pleasures." He draped the towel over the back of a chair and stood with his arms crossed, facing Rip, Julio and Carlos. "Gentlemen, perhaps you would care to join us?"

"I'm more interested in a siesta," Carlos said.

Julio stood and stretched. "I could use one, as well. If we're to go to the festival tonight, I want to be well-rested and alert in case we encounter trouble."

The two SEALs left the patio. Rip stood. "I suppose I could do with a swim. I'll be right back."

He entered the hacienda, glancing back at the sound of a splash.

Hector surfaced next to Tracie, close enough to touch.

Rip's blood heated. He was tempted to turn around and jump into the pool fully clothed to put a little space between Hector and Tracie.

For a long moment, he clenched his fists and counted, reaching fifty before he finally calmed enough to enter the house. He strode across the living area and ran up the stairs taking the steps two at a time, not slowing until he reached the bedroom he shared with Tracie.

He riffled through the drawers, digging deep, searching for swim trunks. After the first two drawers, he was throwing shirts, shorts and underwear on the floor, grinding his teeth down to the nub. Where the hell were his swim trunks?

Finally, he reached the bottom of the shorts drawer and unearthed what was nothing more than a pair of shiny black men's underwear.

"Really, Hank? Real men don't wear tiny swim briefs unless they're competing in a swim competition." He flung the offending item on the bed and dug through the next drawer. None of the shorts would do. As soon as they got wet, they'd be sheer.

"I'm not wearing that," he grumbled. The image of Tracie laughing into Hector's face flashed in Rip's mind and he grabbed the swimwear, shucked his trousers and yanked the garment up over his thighs. He might as well be swimming naked.

He stood in front of the mirror, his cheeks hot, and almost ditched the entire idea. If not for the thought of Hector flirting with Tracie, he would have. Grabbing a towel from the bathroom, he wrapped it around his waist and ran back down the stairs and out to the pool.

Tracie and Hector glanced up as he skidded to a halt at the edge.

"Join us, sweetheart, the water's wonderful." Tracie stood in water that came up to just beneath her breasts, the reflection of sunlight emphasizing the hot-pink bikini top.

"*Si.* Join us Senor Gideon."

"Oh, Hector, we don't need to be so formal. Call him Chuck."

He smiled at Tracie, his charm turned up full blast and then he faced Rip and dipped his head. "Join us, Chuck." His emphasis on Chuck made it almost sound like an insult.

With both of them watching his every move, Rip didn't want to remove the towel. "I think I'll enjoy the sunshine."

"You have to get in. The water is just the right temperature." Tracie batted her eyes at him, making his stomach do all kinds of flips, even knowing she was putting on a show for Hector's benefit. "Please."

The *please* won. With a sigh, he dropped the towel.

Hector's brows rose.

Tracie's green eyes flared and darkened, but she didn't say a word.

Rip dove into the water, figuring that the sooner he got in, the sooner his swimming apparel wouldn't be as conspicuous. When he surfaced, he came up behind Tracie and pulled her against him. "Did you tell Hector where we're going tonight?"

Tracie shook her head. "I thought I'd let you."

Hector's head canted to the side. "Are you going to the festival as planned tonight?"

"We are."

Hector's brows dipped. "It is dangerous for foreigners to wander around the countryside at night. There have been many kidnappings and murders at the hands of *Los Rebeldes del Diablo.* I wish you to reconsider."

Rip smiled and nuzzled the back of Tracie's neck. "My wife has made up her mind."

"What of Senor Delgado?" Hector asked.

"There will be a lot of people in the town. We'll do our best to blend in."

Hector snorted. "Senora Gideon, your skin is far too pale to blend in and Senor Gideon is much taller and broader than most men of the area. I am afraid you will have difficulty getting lost in the crowd."

"That's where your men could come in. Do you mind loaning us the four men you sent with us this morning?" Rip asked. "I need them to dress in clothes that will help them to blend into the crowd. I will have my men do the same. That way if we run into trouble, no one will know they are there to protect us and they can help us get out."

"Oh, sweetie, I do so want to dance. And the decorations were so cute."

Rip shrugged toward Hector. "You see? I can't disappoint my bride."

Hector's frown deepened. "You are putting yourselves in unnecessary danger when you can stay here, behind the walls where you will remain safe."

"But we'll miss the music and the dancing." Tracie leaned toward Hector, though Rip held her back. "We'll be okay. Chuck will be there to protect me, and the other men will be, as well."

Hector shrugged. "So be it. I will inform my men."

"Good. It's all settled. We'll leave at dark." Rip pulled Tracie closer, nibbling the back of her ear. "Now where was I. Ah, yes. I missed you."

She giggled and responded with, "I missed you, too."

Hector's eyes narrowed and he swam away. Lifting himself out of the water, he rose to stand dripping beside the pool.

"Aren't you going to stay?" Tracie asked, her hands resting on Rip's arms, which he'd wrapped around her waist.

"I have business to conduct and I do not intend to be what you call, the third wheel." He nodded to Rip. "Enjoy for as long as you like."

Once Hector left the patio, Tracie squirmed, pushing Rip's hands away. "Let go."

He didn't release her, instead he turned her in his arms and clamped her to him.

"What are you doing?" she whispered, a smile pasted across her angry lips.

"Hector went inside, but I'd bet my favorite snorkel he's standing in the window watching."

Tracie stopped wiggling and sighed. "I supposed you could be right."

"We really need to act more like a newlywed couple," he said. "For the sake of our cover, of course." Rip tightened his hold on her.

"I thought you didn't want to get closer. You don't want to waste your time on a relationship that isn't going anywhere."

"Maybe I've decided to use my indomitable charm to convince you a relationship with me isn't such a bad idea." He brushed his lips across hers. "Now show Hector that we're crazy in love, and you can't live without me."

"You're impossible," she whispered, her wet hands rising to capture his face between her palms.

"No, I'm indomitable. We SEALs—" Rip was cut off by Tracie's lips pressing against his.

She leaned back for a moment to say, "You SEALs talk way too much."

"Only when we have—"

Her mouth descended on his again and her legs wrapped around his waist beneath the water.

For sure now, he wouldn't be able to leave the pool without displaying just how turned on he was by her. At that moment, he didn't care.

He deepened the kiss, pushing past her teeth to slide along the length of her tongue, stroking, caressing and loving every inch of his possession.

Tracie moaned, her thighs tightening, her center rubbing against the front of his swimsuit, igniting a desire so strong, he wanted to take her, there in the pool and to hell with whoever was watching.

"You want me now, don't you?" Tracie nibbled at his ear.

"I've always wanted you."

"Then let's go to our bedroom."

God, he wanted to. More than he wanted to breathe. If they weren't at Hector's house in his pool, and if he wasn't wearing that damned bathing suit, he might have been beyond temptation and carried her into the house and up the stairs to the massive king-size bed and taken her places she'd never dreamed possible.

But they weren't alone. With the possibility that they were being watched, maybe even recorded, Rip knew he couldn't throw caution to the wind.

Tracie had to want to be with him for longer than just the operation. When they were no longer playing the newlyweds, she had to want him to make love to her as much as he wanted to make love to her.

The physical attraction could not be denied. Rip knew there was so much more to life than that and he wanted Tracie to know that, too. If he could find the bastard who'd betrayed her trust, he'd kill him. On the other hand, he was glad she'd met someone who wasn't trustworthy so that when she met someone who was, she'd eventually know the difference.

The sound of someone clearing his throat broke through

the intense and deeply stirring kiss, and Rip tore his mouth from Tracie's long enough to acknowledge the blue-shirted servant.

"Dinner will be served on the hour."

Rip was surprised to see that the sun had begun its descent to the horizon. Shadows had lengthened and darkness would soon settle over the hacienda. After supper they'd load up in the vehicles and return to the little town of Colinas Rocosa and then the adventure would begin.

Hugging Tracie close one last time, he whispered into her ear. "You don't have to come."

She pushed her hands against his shoulders and stared into his eyes. "What are you talking about?"

"Tonight will be dangerous. You can stay here where it's safe and where I won't have to worry about you."

"Look, mister, don't patronize me." She shoved against him, twin flags of color flying her cheeks. "I might not be a SEAL, but I'm just as much a part of this team as Julio and Carlos. More so. I've been on it longer than they have."

"By a day," he pointed out, loving the fire in her green eyes as her ire spiked.

Tracie pushed at his chest. "A day in an agent's life is like seven years."

Rip laughed out loud. "Now you're talking about dogs."

"I mean it. I'm going." She caught his face in her hands and stared hard into his eyes. "Are you listening? I'm going."

"Okay, okay. You're going. But I'm calling the shots. What I say goes. No questions asked. Agreed?" He kissed the tip of her nose.

Her eyes narrowed. "Don't do that. I'm being serious."

"Yeah, me too. Agreed?" He didn't move, refusing to break eye contact. On this, he wouldn't waver. "Agree and go, or refuse and stay behind," he challenged.

She breathed in and blew the air out her nose in a soft snort. "Agreed."

He kissed the tip of her nose again. "You could have agreed with a little more enthusiasm."

"Yeah and you could have asked with a little less force." This time, she kissed the tip of his nose.

He liked it. "Why did you do that?"

She pressed her lips together. "To show you how irritating it is."

"Well, I like it when you're playful."

"Don't get used to it. This operation is almost over."

"Maybe so, but we're not."

"You know how I feel."

"Blah, blah, blah. You're all talk." He scooped her legs out from under her and tossed her into the water.

When she came up sputtering, she slapped at the water, sending a wave square into his face. "That was uncalled for."

"Yeah, and you need to get your dancing shoes on. We leave right after supper."

Her lips twisted in a saucy smile. "I'm not getting out until you do."

Rip cringed at the thought of climbing out of the pool in the package-hugging suit. And his package had been far too inspired by his fake bride. "Fine." Forcing a bravado that was hard to feel wearing such a tiny thing, he hiked his body up on the side of the pool and stood.

Tracie's eyelids drooped and her nipples spiked beneath her bikini top. "You should wear that suit more often. It is totally you."

"Shut up." He dipped his foot in the water and sent a splash her way. "Now hurry up, or I'll leave without you."

"Like hell you will." Tracie pulled herself up out of the water and raced ahead of him for the house, slipping a little on the wet concrete. They ran into the house, laughing all the way up the stairs to their bedroom.

Rip let Tracie hit the shower first, slowing down at the dresser, pretending to select his clothing. The way he felt at that moment, he couldn't continue to resist her and he didn't want to go back on his word. He refused to take her until she admitted there could be something between them on a long-term basis.

Standing at the window, he stared out over the jungle-covered hillside and wondered where he'd be next week and where Tracie would be.

"Hey." A wet washcloth hit him in the side of the head and landed with a splat on the floor.

Rip turned to find Tracie standing in the doorway of the bathroom holding a towel up to her front.

"Aren't you going to join me?" she asked, her voice low and sultry. Then she dropped the towel giving him a full-on view of what she had to offer. She turned and gave him the backside of the same and walked away, leaving the door open, inviting him to follow.

*Holy hell.*

All his good intentions flew out the window and he didn't walk—he ran toward his destiny.

## Chapter Eleven

Tracie ducked under the shower spray, sure she'd gotten to him this time. And she wasn't disappointed when Rip's arms slipped around her middle and pulled her back to his front.

"You play dirty, Agent Kosart."

She leaned into him, letting her head fall back on his shoulder. "I do whatever it takes to get the job done."

"Just because I'm here doesn't mean I've given up."

"It doesn't?" She reached behind her to grasp his hips in her hands and press him closer. "I have you right where I want you."

"And I'm telling you, this isn't over when we leave here."

"Whatever."

He spun her around and into his arms. "Look, Tracie. I don't know what's happening between us. All I know is that I don't want it to end. If you're honest with yourself, neither do you."

She walked her fingers up his chest and chin to press her pointer finger to his lips. "You talk a lot for a man. Shut up and make love to me."

"Not without protection."

Tracie reached behind a washcloth hanging on a rail and produced a foil packet like the ones he'd found in the draw the night before. "Is this what you're talking about? While you weren't a Boy Scout, I made a very good Girl Scout. I make it a point to always come prepared."

Rip laughed out loud. "If you were a Girl Scout, I'm the king of England."

"Well, Your Highness, you're not getting any closer to making use of this royal gift." She tore the edge of the packet with her teeth and removed the contents, rolling it down over his stiff shaft.

Rip scooped her legs out from under her and wrapped them around his waist. He turned, pressing her back against the cool stone tiles and positioning himself at her entrance. But he didn't drive home.

Tracie wiggled, trying to lower herself over him, her body on fire, her core aching with the need for him to fill her. "What are you waiting for?" she moaned.

"You're not ready yet."

"Are you kidding me?" Trying again to take him into her, she gave up and glared at him.

He shook his head. "You're not ready." Then he set her on her feet and wrapped a hand around the back of her neck, tipping her head up to accept his kiss.

He took her mouth in a gentle joining, brushing softly over her lips, sliding into her mouth with his tongue.

Tracie rose on her toes, deepening the kiss, pressing her breasts against his naked chest, wanting to get so much closer to him.

Warm water ran down her back and between them, heating with the fire of their rising desire.

"Please," she moaned.

But he didn't press into her, instead, his lips trailed wet kisses down her chin and the length of her neck to the pebbled tips of her breasts.

Tracie arched her back, urging Rip to take more.

He obliged, sucking her nipple into his mouth, rolling it around on his tongue.

Tracie's body undulated to the rhythm of Rip's tongue. When he nibbled at her, she cried out and clasped the back of his head, forcing him to take more of her breast into his mouth.

When he'd finished with one, he moved to the other and paid it equal attention.

Everywhere Rip touched her, her body burned, her skin was so sensitive it rippled as he moved down her body, skimming across her abs.

He dropped to one knee on the shower tiles and parted her folds with his thumbs.

Tracie sucked in a deep breath and flattened her palms against the tile as he slid his tongue along the strip of flesh packed with a fiery bundle of nerve endings, each popping off a fresh round of sensations through her body.

Her belly clenched and her core heated, aching for him to fill her.

"Damn you, sailor," she said through clenched teeth. "Come to me now."

"Almost there," he muttered, blowing a stream of warm air against her heated center, while water dripped over his head and shoulders.

Only she couldn't concentrate past the tongue flicking, licking and sliding over her, drawing her taut like a fully extended bow string.

"I can't...take...any...more." One more touch of his magic tongue launched her over the edge, spinning her out of control. Her body jerked and spasmed as she shot into the stratosphere, tumbling past the moon in a passion-filled flight to the stars.

Still, he wouldn't let up his attack on her senses, bringing her to a frenzied pitch before she fell back to earth.

"Now." Grabbing his ears, she dragged him up her body. "Take me now," she demanded in a desperate, gravelly voice she didn't recognize.

Rip lifted her again, wrapping her legs around him, positioning his member at her entrance. He paused, his breathing ragged, his face tense. "Say you'll see me again stateside."

"Now?" she wailed.

"Say it." He nudged her but refused to enter.

"For the love of Mike!" She pounded her fists on his shoulder. "Take me."

"Not until you say it."

"Fine! I'll see you stateside."

"A date," he insisted.

"A date." She squeezed her legs around his middle and lowered herself as he thrust upward.

They came together in a rush, her channel slick and ready.

Past the point of impatience, Tracie rose and fell, trying to set a fast-paced rhythm.

Rip growled and backed her against the shower wall. With one hand he pinned her wrists above her head. With the other hand, he held her steady while he slammed into her, over and over, picking up speed with every thrust.

Tracie whimpered, feeling herself climbing that slippery slope again, her body tensing with the promise of another shot at ecstasy.

One last thrust and she pitched over the edge.

Rip released her wrists and held her hips in both hands, buried as deeply as he could go, his member throbbing against the walls of her channel.

When Rip finally moved, he pressed his forehead to hers. "You drive a hard bargain," he whispered, his voice unsteady.

"Me?" she laughed, feeling light and satiated. "You were the one doing all the driving."

He breathed in and let go of the breath in a long, shaky sigh. Then he slapped her naked bottom. "We'd better hurry. Dinner will be on the table and Hector will be waiting for us to appear."

Rip lifted her off him and set her on her feet.

Tracie was glad he didn't let go immediately as her legs could barely support her. She laid her cheek on his chest, listening to the rapid beat of his heart. With a smile, she realized he'd been as affected as she was.

When she could stand on her own, he let go, discarded the condom, shampooed her hair and then his, and pulled her under the shower's spray to rinse all the soap off her head and body.

In quick efficient movements he switched off the water and toweled her dry, then himself.

Feeling as limp as a wet noodle, Tracie let him, enjoying the swift vigor with which he ran the towel over her body, between her thighs and across her breasts. Her body responded to his touch her core heating all over again.

"Do we have to go to dinner?" she asked, her fingers skimming over his shoulders.

He took her hands in his, closing his eyes for a moment as if gathering his wits. "Sadly, yes. I came to Honduras to find a traitor. A man who was responsible for the deaths of a DEA agent and one of my SEAL brothers. I'd love to spend the rest of the night making love to you, but duty comes first."

Tracie pushed back her rising desire. "You're right. Duty comes first." She twirled her towel into a tight twist and popped his thigh with it. "Get moving Mr. Gideon, you're taking your bride out on the town to dance."

RIP GLANCED AROUND at the colorful clothing and decorations lit up by twinkle lights in the middle of the town square of Colinas Rocosa. At one end of the square stood an old Spanish-style church that probably dated back to the early 1800s. The buildings on the other three sides of the square were dingy, chipped stucco structures that had seen better days. But tonight with the cheerful lights and the happy crowd spinning and dancing to the music from a local mariachi band, the place was somewhat magical.

Or would have been if they weren't on full alert watching for Carmelo Delgado's men to appear.

Rip spotted Carlos, Julio and the four men Hector had provided dressed to fit in with the crowd. Although the SEALs looked like the locals in most respects, the breadth of their shoulders made them stand out. Hector's men came closer to fitting in. Though they were rugged, they hadn't spent much time lifting weights or even working hard in the local fields to bulk up.

Rip had Carlos instruct them to take up positions at the four corners of the town square where a live band entertained the festival attendees.

"Come on, good-looking, dance with me." Tracie grabbed his hand and dragged him into the middle of the crush of people. The tune was lively like the six other tunes she'd insisted he dance to. He liked to dance all right, and so far, Delgado and his thugs hadn't made a showing.

Their efforts to find the one responsible for the weapons sales had reached an impasse. If they weren't able to tag one of Delgado's men with a tracking device tonight, they'd have to pay another visit to his plantation and hope to get close enough to tag one there.

Or they could sneak in at night and interrogate Delgado himself. He appeared to have some authority over the men who'd carried the illegally purchased weapons.

Tracie danced close, wrapped her arms around his neck and leaned in. "Anything?"

If she meant was he feeling anything, that would be a big fat yes. Mainly her body against his. If she meant had he seen anything of Delgado, which he was sure was what she'd meant, then… "No."

Tracie danced away from him, her bright red, layered skirt swirled out around her legs. She'd told him of the black jeans she'd worn rolled up beneath the skirt, but even as she twirled, they weren't visible to him or others. On her feet, were a pair of black ankle-high boots. Though most people wouldn't think the boots went with the dress, Rip thought they were damned sexy and could imagine them wrapped around his waist.

He grabbed her hand and twirled her around and back into his arms.

When the song came to an end, another song began immediately. Tired and thirsty, Rip tugged Tracie's hand and led her to the edge of the crowd. "Do you want me to find you a bottle of water?"

Her eyes widened, a faint sheen of perspiration made her pretty face glow. She wore very little makeup and her face had that open, earthy look that reminded him of the great outdoors and wide-open spaces. With her hair hanging loose around her shoulders, Tracie looked like a young girl barely out of her teens.

Rip knew better, though. She was a seasoned, former FBI agent bent on going after truth and justice for Hank Derringer's Covert Cowboys, Inc. And she wore the red skirt just as beautifully as the pretty village girls.

She smiled up at him and then her happy glow faded, her

gaze shifting to a point behind him. "Isn't that Delgado?" she asked.

Without appearing too obvious, Rip eased around to stand beside her. As soon as he did, he could pick out the large, gray-haired Honduran. "Yup. That would be Delgado."

He had one of his men on either side of him and several bringing up the rear.

People moved out of his way as he stepped into the square, either because of the heavy scowl on his face or the fact his men carried semiautomatic weapons.

"Looks like he spotted us," Rip confirmed.

Tracie forced a smile of welcome to her lips and spoke through her teeth. "Get ready. He doesn't appear to be very happy."

"Probably still mad that we eluded his thugs." Rip pushed his lips up into a smile and held out his hand in greeting to the older man.

Delgado took it, but didn't shake it. "What are you doing here?"

Rip grinned wider. "We're here for the festival and the dancing. My wife loves to dance."

"You should have left when you still could," Delgado warned.

"I'm not good at taking orders." Rip continued to smile even though his jaw strained under the effort. "You need to understand that if we're going to be doing business together."

Delgado's brows rose and his men pushed closer. "I have not agreed to do business with you."

"Then I'll go around you to the man in charge. I'm only here for a day. Two, max. If you are not the authority I need to speak to, I'll have to ask you to take me to him."

Delgado snorted. "That is not possible."

"Then we have nothing to talk about." Rip snapped his fingers.

Carlos and Julio moved in behind Delgado's men and jammed pistols into their backs. In Spanish, Carlos warned them not to move or they'd blow holes in them.

Delgado reached for his waistband.

Before he could get there, Rip had pulled the small, but deadly HK .40 from the hidden holster around his own waist beneath the loose-fitting shirt he'd worn. "I wouldn't do that."

"I have many men at the festival. You will not get away," Delgado practically growled.

"I bet I will." Rip, still holding his hand, twisted Delgado's arm and spun him, pinning the older man's arm up between his shoulder blades. "Now, tell your men to back off. You and I will be going for a ride.

Tracie leaned close to Rip. Out of the corner of his eye, he could see her drop one of the small tracking devices into the back pocket of Delgado's pants.

A nod from Carlos and Julio indicated they, too, had dropped their devices in the pockets of their targets.

The music had stopped and the festival goers, their eyes wide and frightened, had backed away from the confrontation taking place in the square, whispering to each other. Some herded the women and children down side streets.

Unwilling to put the good citizen's in danger, Rip knew he had to get Delgado out of the square and away from town before he let him loose. "Take their weapons," he ordered.

Julio and Carlos took Delgado's guards' weapons while Tracie grabbed Delgado's nine-millimeter pistol.

"Tell your other men to stay back or I'll shoot you," Rip said.

Delgado hesitated.

Rip shoved his arm up higher and goosed him with the tip of his gun. "Do it."

Delgado shouted in Spanish.

Carlos snarled. "He's telling them to shoot us." He swung his fist, hitting Delgado in the mouth.

Delgado spit blood out and glared at Carlos.

"You plan on dying tonight, don't you?" Rip jacked his arm up higher behind his back.

The old man cursed. "Okay!" He spluttered in Spanish.

Carlos nodded. "That's more like it. He told them to stay back."

"Let's go." Rip led the way, pushing Delgado in front of him to a location just outside of the small town. They'd parked the vehicles behind a rundown building that appeared to have been abandoned.

Hector's men closed in behind Rip, Tracie, Carlos, Julio and their charges. Delgado's other men followed at a distance.

Rip got into the backseat of the Jeep with Delgado. With nowhere else to sit, Tracie sat in Carlos's lap.

If he'd had a free hand, Rip would have knocked the grin off Carlos's face. Since there was no other choice, he kept his mouth shut and retained his grip on Delgado's arm.

The two other men Carlos and Julio had disarmed were released and told to go back to town. They stood still, hesitant to leave their leader.

Delgado shouted for them to leave.

Without a pause, they turned and ran back to the other men carrying weapons.

Rip had Carlos tell Hector's men to go ahead of them, giving them a good lead before Julio pulled out on the road. Once again, they headed out of town, fully expecting to be followed.

Three miles out, Julio pulled to the side of the road.

Carlos handed Rip a roll of duct tape, which he quickly wound around Delgado's wrists behind his back.

"My men will kill you," Delgado warned.

Rip didn't respond, just slapped a length of tape over the rebel leader's mouth and shoved him out of the Jeep onto the road. As the man struggled to break his bonds, Tracie slipped into the backseat and Julio pulled away.

Once on the road again, Julio hit the accelerator, putting as much distance as possible between them and Delgado. The rebel's men would not be far behind them.

When they'd gone a good mile along the twisting turning roads, Julio announced, "Lights out in one minute."

Rip leaned toward Tracie. "Close your eyes, let them adjust to the darkness." Following his own advice, Rip closed his eyes and waited the minute.

"Lights out," Julio announced. A click indicated Julio had switched the lights off.

Rip opened his eyes. Julio would be half-blinded, having closed one eye for the minute prior and could manage to drive while his other eye adjusted to the limited light provided by the stars above.

Before they'd left Hector's place, Rip had Julio pull the wiring on the Jeep's tail and brake lights as well as the lights to the dash. In purely blackout mode, they drove through the night another three miles before pulling off the road into a copse of trees and brush.

Once again, the men climbed out of the Jeep and covered their tracks with vegetation.

Tracie got out of the Jeep and pulled her skirt off. Her legs below her knees glowed white in the night until she unrolled her black jeans.

Rip handed out camouflage sticks and they went to work covering every pale inch of exposed skin.

The roar of an engine alerted them to an approaching vehicle.

Rip pushed his way up to the edge of the bushes where he could peer through as a truck loaded with Delgado's men rumbled past.

One hundred yards down the road, they slowed, their taillights burning bright red, lighting the darkness.

"Are they turning around?" Tracie asked, having moved silently up behind him. She'd pulled her hair back in a ponytail and her face was completely covered in camouflage paint, only her eyes and teeth shone white.

"I don't know. They stopped." He lifted a pair of night-vision goggles to his eyes and focused on the truck. The red taillights glowed bright. After a moment he could see men dropping to the ground, carrying weapons and spreading out. Some of them moved ahead of the vehicle, others ran back the way they'd come. Toward the spot where they'd hidden the Jeep in the brush. Each man carried a flashlight, the beams crisscrossing along the edges of the road.

"They're headed this way." Rip backed away from his vantage point, took Tracie's hand and led her away from the road.

The Jeep had been parked behind a bunch of tree trunks surrounded at the base by a thick weave of vines. As long as Delgado's men didn't walk very far into the woods, they'd be all right.

Rip led Tracie to a thick bush. Together, they crouched behind it, pulling leafy vines over their backsides.

As Rip glanced around, he couldn't see Julio or Carlos. Trained SEALs wouldn't be visible to the naked eye. Only night-vision goggles, more commonly called NVGs, could pick them out of the darkness by reading their heat signature.

Footsteps crunched on gravel too close for Rip's comfort.

Tracie's hand squeezed his and they hunkered low, careful not to make a sound.

A shout rose up from the direction of the truck. An engine revved and headlights flooded the road, moving back toward Rip and his team.

He held his breath until the truck came to a halt near the point they'd left the road.

In the light, he could see a man crouching close to the ground, his hand skimming across the gravel.

A shout in Spanish made the man jerk to his feet. Others ran toward the truck. In a moment, they had all piled into the truck bed and the vehicle took off, headed back toward the small town.

Not until the taillights disappeared in the distance did Rip let go of the breath he'd been holding.

"That was close," Tracie said, laughing shakily.

Still holding her hand, Rip stood and pulled her to her feet and into his embrace. He kissed her black-painted lips and set her at arm's length. "Did I tell you how sexy you look in black lipstick?"

She kissed him again, leaving some of the black paint on his lips. "Same to you, frogman."

He hugged her close, loving the way she felt in his arms. Then, setting her aside, he clapped his hands together, ready to get the show on the road. "Now all we have to do is wait until they go to their hidden camp in the jungle."

"What makes you think they will?" Tracie asked.

"They were attacked and bested. If Delgado is the leader, he'll go for reinforcements. If he's just a pawn, he'll have to report to the leader. Either way, they will go to the camp tonight and we'll find them."

## Chapter Twelve

The bright green blips that had been moving for the past half hour had stopped. After Delgado's men had loaded up and passed through the small town hosting the fiesta, Tracie, Rip, Carlos and Julio followed. They skirted Colinas Rocosa's outskirts, careful to avoid any men Delgado might have left behind to watch out for them.

Stopping five miles short of their destination, Rip contacted Hank on the sat phone so that he could pinpoint where they were and tell them if there was a better route into the camp. Fortunately, a river close to where they'd pulled off the road also came within five hundred yards of the camp. They managed to get close enough to the river to unload what they'd need to stage their infiltration op.

Rip had given the handheld tracking device to Tracie to monitor while he, Julio and Carlos pulled the inflatable raft and the mini motor out of the rear storage area of the Jeep.

Tracie slipped her arms into one of the bulletproof vests Hank had included in the care package he'd sent with Carlos and Julio. She wore it over the long-sleeved black T-shirt she'd put on.

While the men spread the rubber boat out, Tracie collected an array of smoke grenades and clips full of nine-millimeter bullets, stuffing them into her pockets or strapping them to the vest. When she'd set out earlier that evening, she'd strapped a nine-millimeter Glock to her thigh beneath her party skirt. It was just like the one she'd used when she'd been part of the FBI, and she'd qualified as an expert with a similar weapon on numerous occasions. When she had to use it, the gun felt like an extension of her hand.

Carlos stared down at the small raft, shaking his head woefully. "It's not a RIB."

"What's a RIB?" Tracie asked.

"Rigid hull inflatable boat, one of the boats we use in the Navy," Rip answered.

Carlos pulled what appeared to be a small engine out of the rear compartment of the Jeep and attached it to the back of the raft. "Nor does it have a 470-horsepower engine. I'd give my right arm for one of those right now."

Julio snorted. "You call that trolling motor an engine? My electric toothbrush has more power than that."

"Hey, that trolling motor will be quiet and get us close to the camp without driving in by roads sure to be lined with sentries." Rip nodded toward the river. "We'll be going up river to get in."

Carlos groaned. "Which will make it even slower."

"Yeah. And faster when we leave," Rip reminded them.

"I don't like it." Julio kicked the boat with his boot. "I feel like a kid going fishing, not a man about to sneak into an enemy camp full of angry men with guns. Can't we call in SBT-22 for a little backup?"

Rip's chest tightened. "No."

Tracie stepped in. "Hank didn't brief you on Rip's status?"

Carlos shook his head. "Just that he had been a member of SBT-22. He didn't say why he wasn't a member anymore."

"Because I'm dead," Rip said, his voice flat. He pushed

past the two SEALs and mounted the trolling motor on the back of the boat.

Carlos's brows came together. "How can you be dead when you're standing right in front of me?"

Tracie waited for Rip to answer for himself. When he didn't, she filled the silence. "His unit thinks he was killed by a sniper who wanted him dead because of the information he received from a DEA agent. The agent had been undercover, embedded in the terrorist training camp we're about to enter."

"Holy crap," Julio said. "And here I thought we were going into a cakewalk. Terrorist training camp? Not just some local boys playing at being rebels?"

Carlos's lips spread in a smile. "You said it would be dangerous."

"It will be." Rip faced Tracie. "Now's the time to change your mind."

"I'm going." Tracie helped Carlos load the boat with every bit of equipment they'd brought with them in the Jeep. Weapons, smoke grenades, explosives and detonators.

Rip faced his SEAL brothers. "The same goes for each of you. If you're not comfortable with the mission, there's no shame in backing out. You didn't know what you were going into."

"Can't let a girl show me up." Carlo's lips quirked upward. "Besides, you know the code. The only easy day was yesterday. Let's get wet."

Rip held out his hand to Julio who gripped his forearm instead. "I could use a little exercise. Dude, let's rock and roll."

Tracie climbed into the boat first, then Julio and Carlos.

"We're going in to collect information, not to engage," Rip reminded them as he pushed the boat off the short and hopped in. "We'll stop short of the camp and go in on foot. We can wait until the camp is asleep before we make our move."

The moon was nothing more than the tip of a fingernail in the sky, leaving the stars to provide all the light they needed.

Keeping close to the narrow river's edge and the inky shadows of the overhanging trees, they traversed upriver in the direction the tracking devices indicated.

The going was slow, but then, they weren't in much of a hurry. Delgado's arrival in the camp would get everyone stirred up. They'd need time to wind down again before Tracie and the team of SEALs could slip in, gather what information they could and get out.

"Anything else you want to tell us now that you have our full attention?" Carlos questioned.

Rip, his hand on the till continued in silence for a moment before answering. "I think whoever is selling the weapons to the terrorists is American and could be connected high up the food chain."

Carlos turned to look at Rip in the light from the stars. "Are you kidding me? You think someone in Washington is dirty?"

"I'd bet my best rifle on it," Rip said. "Whoever it is got to our gunnery sergeant and bribed him to leak information about our mission. That leak got a sniper positioned outside the camp. When we brought out the DEA agent, the sniper took out the agent and got one of our men as collateral damage."

"I'd heard about that. A kid named Gosling," Julio said. "Damned shame." Julio and Carlos hung their heads in deference to their lost comrade.

Tracie sat in silence. The SEALs had a strong bond, even though they hadn't known each other before they'd met at Hector's. From all she'd read, their training was so intense, it reinforced the notion to look out for your own and do whatever it took, no matter what, to get the job done.

Tracie was in good shape, but by no means as ruggedly fit as the men who made it through BUD/S training.

Rip aimed the craft toward an overhanging tree, slowed the boat and cut the engine. The remaining momentum sent them toward shore where the rubber hull bumped soundlessly against mud and roots.

Without waiting to be told, Julio and Carlos jumped out of the boat and dragged it up on the shore beneath the drooping tree.

Tracie scrambled out and gathered whatever weapons she could, handing them to the men, one at a time. They all pulled on helmets rigged with communication devices and NVGs.

Rip turned on his radio and waited while the others did the same. Then he spoke softly, "Check."

Through the crackling of the static that erupted in Tracie's ear, she could make out Rip's word clearly. "Check," she repeated.

Rip nodded.

"Check," Carlos and Julio each said and waited for Rip to indicate he'd heard them.

With the handheld GPS tracker in hand, Rip took the lead, heading east, away from the river.

"Remember where we parked," Carlos whispered.

An answering chuckle helped ease Tracie's tension as they pushed through thick foliage, working their way toward the location where the green lights had stopped.

Rip led the way, moving as swiftly as the jungle would allow. The canopy, high overhead, blocked most of the light from the stars, which meant it also blocked a good portion of the sunlight, needed for vegetation to grow at ground level. Other than the occasional vine with huge leaves, they had it pretty easy. The NVGs helped them navigate through the dark forest floor.

Tracie followed Rip, glad she was in good shape as he moved quickly, barely slowing down to catch his breath. Carlos followed her and Julio brought up the rear.

After fifteen minutes of steady forward movement, Rip held up his fist and came to an abrupt halt.

Tracie had been following so closely, intent on keeping up, she nearly plowed into him.

"Get down," Rip whispered through the headset.

All four of them crouched in the underbrush, inching forward, abreast with Rip.

Through her NVGs, Tracie saw the green blobs of people moving about in a clearing a hundred yards ahead.

"I count ten," Rip said.

"I had eight," Carlos replied. "We'll go with your number."

"Looks like they're unloading a big crate from the back of that truck." Rip touched her arm. "Do you see it?"

Tracie could make out six men heaving a huge crate out of the back of what appeared to be an old army two-ton truck with two men seemingly supervising.

"Watch where they take it. I'll bet that's where we need to go," Rip advised.

Tracie riveted her attention on the men moving the crate. For a moment, they disappeared behind the truck. She could see the green outlines of their legs beneath the truck bed and they appeared on the other side, heading toward what looked like a tent. Then they disappeared inside. Through the canvas, Tracie could see the smudge of light green silhouettes moving about.

"Heads down," Carlos said quietly and flattened himself to the ground.

Out of the corner of her NVGs Tracie saw a big green

blob not ten feet from where they crouched on the ground. She eased down to her belly, making herself as much a part of the jungle floor as she could.

"Damn, he's got NVGs," Rip said quietly.

Tracie held her breath, waiting for all hell to break loose.

The man passed by their location and continued on, making a turn at the far end of camp. He had his NVGs tilted upward. A lucky break for their little party. Tracie released the breath she'd been holding and started to rise to her knees.

"Stay put," Rip said. "There's another one coming."

The next man didn't have NVGs but he carried what looked like an automatic weapon with a long banana clip.

Once again, Tracie sucked in a breath and held it. The man headed their way was closer than the first and he kicked at leaves as he walked, appearing bored and slightly resentful at having to pull guard duty.

"We'll stay here until the camp settles." Rip lay on his belly, probably conserving his strength.

Tracie lay as flat as she could, but her heart pounded so hard, she would be worn out before they moved into the camp. Inhaling, she eased the air out of her lungs, willing her pulse to slow. After a few minutes, she had control of her excitement.

SHE WASN'T SURE how long they waited, an hour, maybe two, before the camp grew quiet, the vehicles' engines had cooled and the camp residents had stopped moving around. All except the men pulling guard duty.

Rip rose to his knees. "I'm going to get closer. Everyone stay here until I give you orders otherwise."

"But—" Tracie started.

"You promised to do as I say," Rip reminded her.

"Yes, but—"

"Then don't argue."

She clamped her lips shut. Carlos and Julio hadn't argued. Feeling like a child who had been reprimanded, Tracie lay back down and watched as Rip low crawled into camp.

She didn't like the idea of him going in alone. What if he ran into trouble? Who would have his six?

No one.

For an excruciatingly long time, she lay counting the seconds. Rip hadn't said a word, hadn't let them know he was okay and most of all, hadn't told them to join him.

The only thing that made her feel better was that camp was still quiet, no one had raised an alarm. So, Tracie waited as instructed, chewing a hole in her lip, praying Rip was all right.

RIP MADE IT all the way to one of the tents without incident. So far so good. He was glad he'd made the others wait in the woods. Infiltrating the inside perimeter with one person was hard enough. Taking four in would be impossible. A guard had been deployed outside the tent he'd identified as the one that could contain the evidence he was looking for. The man had started his sentry duties standing and had eventually squatted and then sat. Now his head was tipped forward and he snored with a light whistling sound.

When he was certain nothing was moving, Rip eased his way around the outskirts to the back of what he had tagged as the supply tent. Slipping his knife from his boot, he slit a one-foot long gash in the canvas and pushed it aside, peering in through his NVGs, while his ears perked for any sounds from behind.

Nothing moved inside the tent and it was filled with crates and boxes stacked three deep in some places. Careful not to make a sound, he crawled beneath the canvas and into the tent. Using the crates for cover, he eased his way to the front of the tent to confirm that the tent was empty of personnel.

Near the entrance, one of the crates was set aside, the lid loose on top.

Rip listened for the whistling sound of the guard snoring. For a long moment, he heard nothing, then the soft whistle came to him through the canvas.

Careful not to make a sound, he eased the lid off the crate, lifting it toward the entrance, propping it up to block any light he might have to shine down into the crate.

As dark as it was outside, it was even darker inside the tent. The NVGs only did so much. He had to see more. Shifting the goggles upward he shone a red penlight into the crate. Clothes and cans of vegetables lay jumbled on top. As he dug deeper, his fingers hit the cold metal and hard plastic of M4A1 carbine rifles.

Easing one out of the crate, he laid it on top of the clothing and held the pen over it, clicking the end to take a photo. Looking closer, he saw that the weapons didn't have serial numbers on them.

On the manufacturing plate where they usually were, the metal was smooth, as if it had been ground down and repainted, the paint color a slightly different shade from the rest of the stock. Even the horse emblem identifying the manufacturer had been removed. It wasn't a clone of the M4A1, it was the real deal, modified to hide that fact.

If this was all they had to go on, they didn't have anything.

Disappointed, Rip laid the weapon back in the box and moved the lid back in place. As he settled the wood over the crate, his fingers slipped and the top landed with a soft whomp.

The guard outside the tent flap door, snorted awake, muttering curse words in Spanish.

Rip ducked behind a large wooden crate just as the tent flap was thrown aside.

Peeking through the gap between two crates he could see the guard enter, weapon first. He shone a flashlight around the interior, pausing on the crates behind which Rip hid.

His breath caught in his throat, Rip froze.

A shout went up outside and the guard spun and ran out of the tent.

As soon as the tent flap fell in place, Rip leaped to his feet and ran to the doorway, edging the flap to the side enough he could see what was going on.

A truck rumbled into the camp, headlights illuminating all the tents. A dozen men emerged, rubbing sleep from their eyes and carrying some of the weapons supplied from the crates.

Delgado hurried by Rip's tent, shouting orders. He had to have come from one of the tents next to the one Rip was in. Only three tents had been erected on this side of the compound. One on the very end and four across from where he hid. He could see the one on the end, but not the ones beside him, narrowing the possibilities.

While the men gathered around the truck, Rip slipped out the hole he'd cut in the back of the supply tent and ran to the one beside it, hoping to find any information regarding the shipment of weapons—a cargo manifest, contact name of the shipper, anything that would help them trace the weapons back to the seller. He tried to listen for any sounds of movement inside the tent, but the commotion outside drowned out anything inside. As he inserted his knife to tear a hole, he prayed the noise from the truck engine was sufficient to mask the sound of ripping canvas.

When he had a gap big enough, he lifted the flap and

peered inside. Half a dozen pallets were spread across the floor along with clothes hanging from a line struck from pole to pole. It appeared to be the equivalent of a portable barracks for the terrorists who trained there.

Delgado held more of position of authority than a lowly grunt.

Rip moved on to the next tent. A loud crash and the sound of splintering wood sounded in the center of the compound, a man cried out and others shouted all at once. Whatever they were unloading from the truck must have crashed onto one of the men.

The confusion would be enough to allow him to check out the next tent. Quickly, he moved into position behind the next tent, slit a tear in the back and peered inside. A make-shift desk had been erected with paper scattered across the top. A cot stood in the corner with mosquito netting hanging from the roof down over the cot. Nothing moved inside the tent.

Rip crawled through the hole and, keeping low, moved toward the desk. Quickly, he snapped pictures of the documents, one after the other until he had all of them. He found a battered briefcase on the floor beside the desk and flicked the clasps open.

A moan behind him made him freeze. He turned to find a woman lying among a pile of blankets on the floor of the tent. She lifted her head and frowned at him in the dim light that shone through the canvas from the truck outside.

"Who are you?" she asked in groggy Spanish.

He replied in Spanish. "No one, go back to sleep."

Her frown deepened. "You are not Carmelo." She straightened, pulling the blankets up over her naked body.

Her scream sliced through the night, piercing Rip's eardrums.

Throwing the briefcase in front of him, he dove for the

slit in the back of the tent, managing to get through before the first man entered the tent behind him. He scooped up the briefcase and ran as fast as he could, the darkness hampering his progress and making him second-guess where he was going. Keeping the light from the truck in his peripheral vision, he circled the camp, watching for the men guarding the perimeter.

The screaming didn't stop until he was halfway around the camp. He heard a shout near the point he'd left Tracie, Carlos and Julio and prayed they hadn't been discovered.

Hunkering low, he moved more slowly toward their position. Before he got within fifty yards, the whole world erupted in a fiery explosion.

## Chapter Thirteen

When the truck lumbered into the camp, Tracie could no longer stand by and do nothing. "What if he's trapped somewhere that he can't get out without alerting them to his presence?" she whispered to Carlos.

"He will get out."

"We could set up a diversion just in case." Julio patted the plastic explosives he had tucked into his vest earlier.

"No." Carlos remained firm. "He'll let us know if he needs help."

Julio pointed to a beat-up van parked near the edge of camp, closest to them. "I could be there, set a charge and get back before Rip returns. And no one will see me."

Carlos shook his head, the movement slowing as if he was considering the suggestion. "Remote detonation? I don't want to kill our guy."

A cold chill slithered down the back of Tracie's neck, in direct contrast to the sweat dripping off her brow. "I say let Julio go for it." She positioned her nine-millimeter in front of her. "I've got your back."

Julio stared at her, his brows twisting. "You sure you know how to use that thing?"

"I'll show you just how well if you make another comment like that."

Carlos chuckled softly. "Go."

Julio slipped into the night. Once he left their position, Tracie didn't see him again until he slid beneath the van and then only because she knew he'd be there. The headlights from the truck provided just enough illumination to see when he finished and rolled out from under the chassis.

Back into the night, he moved, virtually invisible until he slipped up behind Tracie and Carlos.

Tracie started, rolled onto her back and aimed her pistol at the man.

On his knees, Julio held up his hands. "It's me. Don't shoot."

"Give me a little warning next time." Her heart hammered against her ribs. "I almost shot you."

Julio lay on the ground between them.

"Did you see Rip?" Tracie half hoped he had and then again that he hadn't. If he'd seen him, how many terrorists would be able to see him?

"No."

A scream rose above the noise of the truck's engine.

Tracie watched as the men behind the truck ran for one of the tents on the other side of the camp.

"We've got trouble," Julio said beside her.

"What now?" Tracie asked.

"The sentry with the NVGs is headed this way. And I don't mean sliding by us, he's headed right for us."

"Back up, slowly, stay low," Carlos warned.

"Damn, he's coming faster," Julio said. "Can I shoot him?"

"No!" Tracie said as quietly as she could. "If we fire a weapon, we alert the others to our presence."

They had backed away several yards when the man headed their way shouted.

Julio stopped moving and pulled out the detonator. "Time to blow."

Tracy and Carlos covered their ears a second before Julio hit the switch.

A loud bang shook the ground and the night sky lit up like the Fourth of July. The sentry hit the dirt and covered his ears.

Carlos dropped his hands from his ears and grabbed Tracie's arm. "Let's move."

The initial explosion was followed by a secondary explosion as the van's gas tank erupted in a fiery ball, spewing fuel into the air, catching the nearby tents and some of the men on fire. Gunshots were fired and the whole camp churned in turmoil.

Carlos tugged Tracie's arm. "Come on!"

She dug her heels into the ground. "Not without Rip."

"He'll come when he doesn't find us where he left us." Carlos dragged her away from the burning camp.

Again Tracie dug her heels in the dirt. "I'm not leaving without him."

A shout sounded behind them.

A bullet whizzed past Tracie's head and hit the tree in front of her. She quit fighting Carlos, dropped to her hands and knees and crawled across the ground. When she reached a massive tree trunk, she rolled behind it for cover.

More shouts rose from the fire at the center of the compound. Fortunately, most of them were battling the blaze and unconcerned about one lonely sentry, fighting a battle all on his own.

Tracie aimed her weapon at the man racing toward them and almost pulled the trigger when a rectangular object flew out of the trees and hit the guerilla in the side of the head.

He slammed against a tree trunk and sank into a heap, the rectangular object skidding to a halt on the ground beside him.

A dark silhouette detached itself from a nearby shadow, bent to scoop up what appeared to be a briefcase and ran toward them.

Her heart pounded even harder—Tracie would recognize that form anywhere.

"Rip!" She staggered to her feet and threw her arms around his neck.

He dropped a quick kiss on her lips and said, "We have to get out of here."

"I'm one step ahead of you, buddy." Carlos raced for the river.

Rip, holding the briefcase in one hand and Tracie's hand in the other, ran after him.

Julio brought up the rear, covering their six.

When they reached the overhanging tree where they'd left the boat, everyone tumbled in while Rip pushed off the shore and settled in next to the motor.

Tracie peeked over the sides and spotted the man Rip had knocked over with the briefcase.

He stood on the shore beside a tree and raised his rifle, letting loose a short burst of bullets. The rounds plunked into the water close to the raft.

"Get down!" Rip cranked the motor, grabbed the till and angled it toward the shadows along the far shore, which wasn't far enough for Tracie's tastes. The rubber raft puttered down the river at the pace of a snail's crawl.

Carlos aimed at the man on the shore and fired, but the pistol's range wasn't nearly as far as that of the M4A1. Their attacker was quickly out of their weapons' range.

More bullets pelted the water and one ripped into the little boat's hull.

Air hissed out of the tear and one of the compartments gradually deflated, slowing the boat even more. Tracie pinched the rubber over the hole in an attempt to slow the collapse. Water trickled into the bottom, but they continued downstream moving farther and farther away from the shooter.

Tracie looked ahead at a bend in the river and prayed they'd get there before another bullet sank them completely.

As they rounded the corner, the shooter fired again, missing the boat.

Rip grunted and hunched forward.

"Rip?" Tracie rose up, grabbed Rip's shoulders and leaned him upright. Her right hand came away warm and sticky.

"I'm okay," he said through gritted teeth. "He just nicked me."

"Yeah, right," Carlos reached into his vest and pulled out a pouch. "That's a self-aid kit. As long as it didn't hit an artery—"

"It didn't," Rip said. "I'm fine."

"As I was saying," Carlos eased his way to the back of the boat. "Apply pressure to the wound to stop the bleeding. I'll take the till."

"I've got it," Rip groused.

"He'll live," Julio said. "As grumpy as he is, he'll live."

"I told you I was fine," Rip forced a tight smile.

"Bull." Tracie tugged at his good arm. "Let Carlos steer or you'll run us into the trees."

Rip let Tracie drag him into the center of the raft. She dug her fingers into the hole in his shirt and ripped it away from his shoulder. Tearing open the pouch Carlos had given her, she found a folded wad of gauze and adhesive tape. "Looks like the bullet went clean through."

"Good," Rip said, his voice tight. "At least they won't have to dig it out."

Tracie pressed a wad of gauze to the front wound and taped it tightly in place. She did the same for the exit wound. When she was done, she used her hands to scoop the rising water and blood out of the boat.

Rip leaned close to her. "Thanks."

"You're welcome. And by the way, you make a terrible patient."

"You make a sexy nurse with black lipstick."

"Well, don't get used to it. I prefer you intact."

He chuckled. "I prefer you the same way." With his lips next to her ear, he whispered, "And naked."

Julio coughed and spluttered. "TMI, buddy. I didn't have to hear that."

Tracie's cheeks burned and she was glad the trees hid them from the starlight at that moment. Carlos steered them into the tiny cove they'd departed from what seemed like days ago and could only have been a few hours.

Leaving the half-sunken raft on the shore, they climbed into the Jeep and headed toward Hector's hacienda, lights out, navigating by the light of the stars.

No one spoke, as if each of them was lost in thought. The operation hadn't gone exactly according to plan. Tracie hoped that whatever they found in the briefcase would help them identify the man selling weapons to the terrorists and shut him down.

Rip faded in and out of consciousness on the way back to Hector's. The bumps and jolts shot pain through Rip's arm, waking him every time Julio darted off the road to hide in the jungle when he spotted other vehicles on the road.

By the time they reached the hacienda, he could barely stand. Julio and Carlos half dragged, half carried him into the house and up the stairs to the bedroom he and Tracie shared.

Hector sent for a doctor and insisted his staff help Rip out of his dirty clothes and into the shower. None of them had had time to wash the camouflage paint from their faces, but Hector refrained from asking about it. He saved his questions until Rip was clean and the doctor had been there to dress his wounds with sterile bandages and give him a tetanus shot.

To have his guests show up with a gunshot wound and looking like terrorists themselves, was a lot to ask of their host without an explanation. Though he was tired and would rather just sleep it off, Rip figured he owed Hector the truth. The man had been more than helpful and patient with them.

Hector stood beside Rip's bed. "If there's anything else you need, just ask. Either I or one of my servants would be more than happy to get it for you." The man turned and would have walked out of the room, but Rip couldn't let him.

"Wait. I need to tell you what's going on."

Tracie had just walked in. "Do you want me to go or stay?"

"Stay," Rip said.

She turned, closed the door and walked across the room to stand on the other side of the bed, facing Hector.

In a few short minutes, Rip laid it out, telling Hector about what had happened when SBT-22 had attempted to extract the DEA agent, the death of his teammate and his own attempted murder in Mississippi.

He brought Hector up to date on what had occurred in the terrorist training camp that evening and why he had a bullet wound and the four of them wore camouflage paint.

"We have to find out who is selling American military weapons to the terrorists and shut them down," Rip ended.

Hector remained silent throughout.

"We understand if you want us to leave tonight," Tracie added. "It's a lot to ask you to harbor people who have stirred up the hornet's nest. And for all we know, we might have what we came for in that briefcase."

Hector pinched the bridge of his nose. "I wish you had been open and honest with me from the beginning."

Rip nodded. "Hank trusted you enough to send us here, but he asked us not to reveal who we were and why we had come. The fewer people who knew about our mission the more likely our cover story would be accepted."

Hector nodded. "I understand." He turned and paced to the door and back. "Had I known, I could have helped much more than just sending four men out with you. I have a boat you could have used. We could have launched an attack that would have taken every one of those murdering bastards out of existence." He clenched his fist, his face contorted into an angry, tortured mask. "They deserve to die for what they did."

Tracie rounded the bed and laid her hand on his back. "We couldn't go in killing everyone there. If we don't have what we need, we might have to capture their leader and extract that information from him."

"You can't interrogate a dead man." Rip gave a tired smile. "They don't have much to say."

The anger seemed to drain out of Hector. "You are correct. It is just as well I was not involved or I might have ruined the mission."

"As it is, they will have to move their camp again. The fire was big enough to be picked up by the satellites." Rip lay back and closed his eyes. "If you need us to leave tonight, we can."

"No," Hector spoke softly. "You are doing my country a service by attempting to stop the flow of weapons into the hands of the terrorists. I want to help in any way I can."

"A good night's sleep is what I need now. In the morning we'll look over what we got and go from there." His blood loss had affected him more than he'd expected and he fought to stay awake.

"I'll leave you two alone." Hector's brows rose. "Unless Senora Gideon, which I'm certain is not your name—" he laughed softly "—would like another room?"

"No," Tracie spoke firmly. "I'm staying with Senor Gideon." She grinned. "I'm getting used to the name and the man. Plus I want to make sure he doesn't bleed all over your bed."

"Do not worry about the bed." Hector opened the door. "Thank you for all you have done." With that he left Tracie and Rip alone, closing the door behind him.

Rip patted the bed beside him.

"I want to get a shower before I go to bed." She pressed her lips to his forehead.

She must have taken off her shoes because he didn't hear her move across the floor. The bathroom door closed and the shower started.

Rip lay back, tired beyond all measure and his shoulder ached, but they were safe and Tracie hadn't been shot or killed in the process of infiltrating the terrorist camp. He'd call that a good day.

## Chapter Fourteen

Tracie hurried through the shower, scrubbing the black camouflage paint from her face, hoping to get back to the bed before Rip fell asleep.

It had been wishful thinking on her part. Still wound up from the explosion, gunfire and hiding in the woods, she knew it would be a while before she was tired enough to sleep. Carlos and Julio had helped get Rip into the house and then gone to their own rooms to rest up for whatever was in store for them the following day.

Tracie slipped into a silk robe and wandered around the room stopping at a small desk set against the wall. The briefcase Rip had used as a weapon lay on the smooth, polished wood. Someone had wiped the exterior clean of the mud it had collected on their race through the jungle.

Sitting at the chair in front of the desk with only the light from the bathroom to see by, she flipped the catches and opened the case.

Before she could peruse the contents, a soft knock sounded on the door. She rose to answer.

Hector stood in the hallway. "I sent twenty of my men to round up as many of the terrorists as they could. We were fortunate and caught Delgado and he is locked up in the cellar of a barn not far from here."

"Good. That will keep him from alerting his supplier that some of his documents are missing."

Although they spoke quietly, Tracie was afraid they'd disturb Rip. "Look, let me bring the case downstairs where we can go through it. Hopefully it will contain something we can use to trace the weapons shipments back to the States."

"I would be honored to help."

Tracie closed the case and carried it from the room and downstairs to Hector's study.

He cleared his massive mahogany desk. Tracie set the briefcase in the middle and flipped it open.

Tracie shuffled through documents and bills of lading, searching for a link between Carmelo and the shipments of weapons, finding only records of food and supplies. She sorted them into stacks. Some were from businesses in Honduras. Others were imports from Costa Rica, Guatemala and the Dominican Republic. Nothing really stood out.

With the briefcase empty, she stared down at it. Something about the case wasn't right. It was much shallower than the exterior would indicate. Not just the difference of the width of the materials used to make the case. There had to be at least an inch and a half's difference.

Tracy felt along the inside lining, dug her fingernail into the fabric and lifted up. The bottom rose, revealing a hidden compartment. "Well, look at this."

Hector leaned over her shoulder. "Delgado is smarter than I expected."

Inside was an array of papers, a passport and an airline ticket for Dulles International Airport for a man named Enrique Perez. The name wasn't familiar to Tracie, but the photograph was of the man Tracie knew as Carmelo Delgado.

"Check this out." She handed the passport and the ticket to Hector.

Beneath the papers lay a thin mobile phone.

Tracie lifted it and pressed the button to switch it on. The screen blinked to life, but it was password protected. "Hector, do you have access to the internet?"

He nodded. "I have satellite connection."

"I need to connect my laptop."

"Anything you need."

Tracie hurried back to the bedroom, checked on Rip and returned with the thin laptop she'd stashed in her suitcase. While she'd been upstairs, she had also claimed the satellite phone Hank had given her. Now that they had some information, she could turn it over to her boss and his computer genius to figure out.

Tracie placed the call. "Hank, it's Kosart."

"Hi, Tracie. How are things going?" Though his voice started out groggy, it cleared quickly. "Did you make it into the terrorist camp?"

"We did. If the spy satellites were over it an hour ago, they should have picked up an image of it. The whole camp was lit up like the Fourth of July."

Hank chuckled. "I take it you made a splash."

"Yes, sir." Her lips quirked. "Julio is amazing with pyrotechnics."

"The Navy does a helluva job training SEALs on demolition. We're lucky to have him on the CCI team," Hank agreed. "Were you able to retrieve any data?"

"We're not sure. My partner managed to snag a briefcase belonging to the leader of the *Diablos*. Unfortunately, during our escape, he took a bullet to the shoulder."

"Is he okay?"

Tracie's gut knotted. "He lost a lot of blood, but Hector brought a doctor in to treat him. He's holding his own."

"Good. He's a good man. We could use more men like him on our team."

Tracie smiled. "I think he already has a job."

"See what you can do to recruit him."

Her heart skittered at the thought of working with Rip in the Covert Cowboys, Inc. The man was a dedicated SEAL. What were the chances of him giving up a life he loved to go to work for a billionaire? The SEALs were a tight-knit community.

But then there was Carlos and Julio, both SEALs who'd decided they'd had enough. Tracie wondered if Rip would do the same. Dragging her thoughts back to the present, she continued, "We found a cell phone in a hidden compartment of the case, but it's password protected."

"Connect the phone to the computer. I'll get Brandon on it right away."

"Already set up and ready for him." No sooner were the words out of her mouth then the cursor moved on the screen even though her hand was nowhere near the touchpad.

"Leave it to Brandon," Hank said. "He'll have it hacked and the numbers downloaded in no time. Anything else?"

"Not much. I'll scan the documents and send them your way to see if you can find a connection to the weapons shipments. Also, Delgado had a ticket to Virginia and a fake US passport under the name of Enrique Perez."

"Scan and send the documents. Brandon's already working on the phone. We'll get back to you as soon as we have anything."

"Roger." Tracie ended the call and looked at Hector. "I don't suppose you have a scanner I could use? I have a portable one, but it will take forever."

"I do." He opened a cabinet next to his desk revealing a state-of-the-art, combination printer and scanner.

For the next hour, Tracie scanned documents and sent

them to Hank. She also downloaded and sent the photos Rip had taken with his penlight camera. When she was done, she stretched and yawned. "I think that's all we can do for now."

Hector nodded. "You might as well get some rest."

"You, too."

"I'd planned to after I check with the men holding Delgado."

Tracie climbed the stairs so tired she could barely lift her feet. The adrenaline high she'd been on was long gone and all she wanted was to lie down and sleep.

Other than a light she'd left on in the bathroom, the massive bedroom was dark. She could make out Rip's form lying so still, she touched his chest to see if he was breathing.

He grabbed her wrist and pulled her down to him. "You smell good," he said, his voice like warm syrup over gravel.

"Better than river water and camo paint?" she whispered, pressing her lips to his forehead.

"I kinda like that scent on you, too. You're pretty hot when you're dressed for battle."

"You weren't so bad yourself." She smoothed a lock of his hair back from his forehead.

"Are you going to stand there all night, or get in bed?"

"I'm afraid I'll hurt you."

"My shoulder's sore, but I'll hurt a lot more if I have to get up and put you in the bed."

"Okay, okay. I'm getting in."

He let go of her wrist, his gaze slipping over her body in the silk robe. "I like that robe on you."

"You'll like what's under it better." Tracie untied the sash and let the garment slip from her shoulders to pool around her ankles to reveal the white teddy.

Rip moaned. "You sure know how to hurt a guy."

"Oh, if this is going to be too much for you…"

"Don't you dare walk away now." When he reached for her, she danced out of range.

"I really don't want to cause you any more pain."

"Come here."

She straddled his hips and lowered herself over him, careful not to touch his injured shoulder as she nuzzled his neck on the opposite side. "I thought maybe I could do all the work this time."

He lifted the hand of his good arm and cupped her cheek. "I'm all for equal opportunity." Then he covered her lips with his, capturing the back of her head to deepen the kiss.

"You scared me tonight." Tracie lay down pressing her ear to his chest, listening to the beat of his heart.

"When I got back to where I left you, I about had a heart attack when you and the team weren't there." His tongue slipped between her teeth, probing her mouth, caressing her in urgent strokes.

"I wouldn't have left without you." She kissed her way down his chest and tongued a dark brown nipple, nibbling on it before she moved to the other.

"You know, I could get used to this," he said.

"Get used to what? Me doing all the work?" She sank her teeth into his skin, biting gently. "Don't. I like it when you're on top."

"No, I could get used to having you around."

She stopped midlick, her heart heavy, her stomach knotting. Then she slid off him to his uninjured side, resting her hand on his chest, her thigh draped over his. Resting her head in the crook of his shoulder, she sighed.

Why was she fighting this so hard? She liked him. He liked her. Their chemistry was off the charts. So why not go with it?

Because it would lead to heartache and Tracie wasn't

sure she was strong enough to have her heart broken again. Especially by this man. Where Bruce had been handsome and exciting, he'd also been a liar and a traitor.

Cord Schafer was a good man, dedicated to his country and the men in his unit. He was a man she could respect and maybe even fall in love with. But the time and distance that would be between them would make anything they might want to have impossible. She didn't want to risk her heart again, but damn. She suspected it was too late.

RIP LAY STILL for a long moment, wishing he'd kept his big mouth shut. Everything had been going so well. She'd worried about him in the thick of things and had been right there, tending his wounds when he'd been shot. Then to come to him in that teddy...

And he had to go and ruin it all by talking about the future.

"Look, I understand how you feel about long-term relationships. I've already told you how I feel about them and that I think we'd be good together."

He pulled in a deep breath and let it out, twinges of pain shooting through his shoulder with every movement. "I promise not to bug you about it again. After nearly dying several times in the past couple months, I've come to the conclusion that maybe I need to loosen up and live in the moment. No expectations, no commitments. What I'm trying to say, and doing a terrible job of it, is that I just want to hold you. When you want me to let go, I will." His arm tightened around her. "I'll take what I can get for as long as I can get it."

Tracie sighed, pressing her lips to his skin. "Thank you." Nestling closer she slipped an arm over his chest. "Much as I'd like to make love to you, it's probably better if you rest. Who knows what Hank will have for us when Brandon decodes the phone."

"Phone?" Rip lifted his head to stare down at Tracie's face. "What phone?"

With her eyes already closed, she yawned and said. "The one Hector and I found in the secret compartment in the briefcase."

"I feel like Rip van Winkle instead of Rip Schafer. Did I miss anything else?"

"Just that Hector collected Delgado and some of his men and is holding them in the basement of a building nearby."

"He did what?" Rip half sat up, pain stabbing through his shoulder. He eased back down, wincing. "Catch me up on that, will you?"

"He sent a large contingent of his men to where the camp had been. Hector's men surprised those of Delgado's men who were still there trying to salvage what they could. Hector's men captured some of them who willingly disclosed Delgado's location. When they got to Delgado, the terrorist leader's men scattered and they were able to capture Delgado."

"Did Delgado talk? Did he tell Hector who sold him the guns?"

"Not a chance." Tracie yawned again and buried her cheek against his side. "Hank will let us know what he finds on the phone."

"Anything else interesting in the briefcase or on my penlight camera?"

"Delgado had a plane ticket and US passport under another name. Hank and his team back in Texas are going over the data."

When Rip opened his mouth to ask another question, Tracie pressed her finger to his lips. "Hank will call when he knows anything. I've told you everything. Now get some rest and regenerate all that blood you lost. We're not done yet, and I'm tired."

He lay still for a while, his good arm curled around Tracie, holding her close. Before long her deep, even breaths blew warm air against his skin. She'd fallen to sleep, wearing that damned teddy and pressing her breasts to his ribs. He was in pain from more than just his shoulder, but he wouldn't wake her. She'd been through as much as he had that day. She needed to sleep.

If Hank's techie was half as good as Tracie said, he'd get something off that cell phone or glean something from the data found in the briefcase.

In the meantime, he would enjoy the moment, holding Tracie as if there would be no tomorrow, only today. And with Tracie, that could be true.

He was out of ideas or ways to convince her that their relationship was worth making the effort for. But he wasn't giving up yet. They had until they resolved this case. He'd take all he could get.

Exhaustion claimed him and he slept, dreaming about explosions, firefights and losing sight of Tracie in the confusion. No matter which way he turned, he couldn't find her. The fire burned high, creeping closer until he saw her standing with her back to the flames, nothing but a faceless silhouette. She reached out to him, but he couldn't quite touch her hand. Just as the fire swept over her, he felt as though his heart would explode, his pulse pounding so hard he heard ringing in his ears.

The ringing continued, growing lower until he surfaced from the dream.

Beside him, Tracie leaned over to the nightstand and made a grab for the satellite phone, knocking it to the floor. She rolled over.

Before he could catch her, she tumbled off the bed, landing on her knees on the carpeted floor, fumbling with the phone until it stopped ringing.

"Yeah." Her voice cracked as she sat cross-legged. She listened for a moment, pushing her hair back from her face. "Sounds like an excellent place to start…Good…We'll be on it." She ended the call and glanced up at Rip. "The plane will be here in less than an hour. Are you up to flying?"

Rip sat up and shoved the sheet aside. He was light-headed and his arm was sore, but he could move. "Where are we headed?"

"Virginia."

## Chapter Fifteen

Tracie stared out over the wing of the Citation as it took off from Hector's grass landing strip.

Carlos and Julio stayed with Hector's team of guards, providing ground support and protection as the airplane rolled down the runway and launched into the sky over the Honduran jungle. Once in the air at a decent cruising altitude, Tracie tapped into the satellite Wi-Fi and connected a live video feed into the Raging Bull Ranch.

Hank Derringer's face filled the screen.

"No problems getting out of the country?" he asked.

"None," Tracie responded. "Hector and his men were invaluable in their support."

"I knew he would be. He's a good man. It's a shame about his family."

An image flashed in her mind of the portrait hanging in the hallway in Hector's hacienda. She was glad the *Diablos* had been crippled by their intel-gathering operation. Anyone who would gun down a six-year-old or condone their men firing on a child was worse than an animal. The leader of the *Diablos* deserved no mercy. But as much as Tracie would have loved to let Hector deal with Delgado, the US government would need to interrogate him.

"As I said earlier, Brandon was able to trace the phone numbers on the cell phone. Most of them were to a disposable phone that was purchased in Virginia. The purchaser used a fake ID and listed a bogus address."

"Then it's a good thing we're headed to Virginia." Tracie said.

Hank grinned. "Fortunately, one of the phone numbers was from a cell phone registered to a Belinda Tate who lives in Alexandria, Virginia. The call didn't last long, only five seconds."

"So why is this Tate woman important?" Rip stood behind Tracie, leaning over so that Hank could see his face on the screen.

She could feel the heat from his body and smell the clean, fresh scent of his aftershave. A thrill rippled the length of her spine and out across her skin in goose bumps.

Hank's eyes narrowed. "She might not be important, but her husband, Vance, is. He works at the Blackburn Gun Manufacturing plant outside of Alexandria."

Tracie sat forward, all thoughts of how good it felt to have Rip leaning over her pushed to the back of her mind. "But the weapons at that terrorist training camp looked exactly like M4A1s they issue to soldiers in the US Army. If I'm not mistaken, Blackburn isn't the manufacturer that makes them."

"And there are plenty of knockoffs," Hank said. "I need you two to infiltrate Blackburn, find out if they are making knockoffs and supplying the weapons. If they are, find out who authorized it."

"From what I saw in that camp, those weapons were the real McCoy, not knockoffs. But their manufacturing plates had been ground off and the stock had been repainted."

"Perhaps that's what Blackburn has been doing. It's up to you two to find out. And, if that's what's happening, we also need to find out how they're getting the guns. Brandon hasn't found any records in their system indicating shipments from the usual government supplier."

"Which means they aren't getting them legally," Tracie concluded.

"Exactly. Let me know what you find and if you need backup." Hank signed off, leaving Rip and Tracie staring at the screen.

"How do you propose we get into Blackburn?" Tracie asked. "Think we could try to sneak in at night?"

Rip shook his head. "They will have that place covered in surveillance cameras."

Tracie tapped a finger to her lip. "We could disable the cameras…"

Rip's gaze locked on the point where her finger touched her lip, his eyes flaring. He swallowed before he answered, "We'd have to find them first."

Tracie's pulse quickened at the way Rip was staring at her lip, and she dropped her hand to her lap. Having him so close and not touching him was hard enough as it was. They had a job to do and the four- or five-hour flight gave them ample time to plan their attack. "How do we get in to check them out?"

Rip's lips spread into a wide grin. "Mrs. Gideon, it's time to arm the security staff around your six-million-dollar home in Costa Rica."

Tracie's brows arrowed into a tight V. "What six-million-dollar home?"

Crossing his arms over his chest, Rip answered, "The one we need to buy arms to protect." He nodded toward the computer. "For a start, we need a home. Do you mind?"

Tracie scooted over one seat and let Rip have the helm of the computer.

His fingers tapped the keyboard, bringing up a search

engine to find real estate in Costa Rica. "What kind of home would you like?"

"I don't care."

After another call to Hank, giving him the bare-bones of their plan, they spent the next hour, combing through high-end homes. Tracie was amazed at how similar their tastes were in the home they finally settled on. It almost made her feel as though they were actually selecting a home they could live in.

She sighed. "It's a beautiful home and who wouldn't love to own it?"

"It's okay, if you have that kind of money. And it's great for our pretend home." He downloaded pictures to the computer and sent them to his cell phone. "It's a good start to consult with a firm about setting up security cameras and arming it with the kinds of weapons we'd need to deter thieves."

"You know, even if I had the money to own something like that, it's still too big." Tracie shrugged. "I'd much rather have a small cabin in the mountains with a stone fireplace."

"I've always loved the Colorado Rockies. I can picture that cabin perched on a hillside with large picture windows, overlooking a mountain valley."

"Flowers in the spring and summer, and snow-covered in the winter." Tracie smiled. "I grew up in West Texas. It's arid and hot there."

"I grew up in Illinois farmland," Rip said. "Not many hills there. Lots of snow, but no mountains. I've always wanted to live where there were mountains."

"But you're a SEAL." Tracie shook her head. "I thought SEALs loved being around the water."

"No doubt about it. I do. But I love the mountains, too." He frowned. "It doesn't matter. I belong to the Navy until I retire or get out."

Tracie sighed. Playing make-believe with Rip was a self-defeating effort. "We do what we have to do and go where we're needed."

"I live where I have to live, because I'm in the military. With you, the sky's the limit. You have choices."

"I work for Hank. I go where he wants me to go."

"But if you wanted, you could live where you wanted to live and deploy from there to where Hank needs you to go."

She narrowed her eyes. "I suppose. But that doesn't mean I'm going to follow a man around the world. My work is just as important to me. I don't ever want to be dependent on a man for my income or identity."

"No one gets that more than I do." Rip cupped her cheek. "I never said I'd expect any woman I was involved with to give up her life to follow me."

"No? But that's what would happen if you wanted any time together when you're not deployed."

Rip's brows drew together. "The personal life of a SEAL is not an easy one. The woman who chooses to get involved with one *needs* to be independent and ready to handle anything. When we deploy, we don't know if we're coming back, much less on our own two feet or in a body bag."

Tracie's chest clenched and her eyes stung. "All the more reason not to get involved with a frogman, if you ask me." Tracie swallowed hard. "What woman would want to sit around twiddling her thumbs waiting for someone to show up on her doorstep announcing her man was dead?"

Rip smoothed the hair back from her forehead. "What about you? You work in a dangerous job. You could be killed by whatever bad guy you're trying to nail for Hank."

"Yeah, but I don't expect a man to stay at home twiddling his thumbs waiting for me to throw a few crumbs of attention and affection his way when I'm home. He'd get bored and go looking for a woman willing to satisfy his needs. I don't want that for either of us."

"Because you had one bad experience with a jerk who took advantage of your affection, doesn't mean you should give up on all of us." He kissed her again. "On me. You don't know what you're going to get out of love until you give it a chance."

"And you're asking me to give you a chance? A man who could come back from a mission in a body bag?" Her words caught on a sob that she choked back.

"No, I'm asking you to give me a chance to see if what we're feeling is more than just lust, which I highly suspect it is. To grab for whatever happiness you can, while you can."

"And when I'm not around, will you grab another woman to find happiness?"

"I told you before, life is too short to waste on one-night stands. I'm in it for the full package." He bent to take her lips in a gentle, coaxing connection that made her heart swell with so much emotion she could barely breathe past it.

Tracie wrapped her hand around the back of his neck and pulled him closer, deepening the kiss, wanting it to go on forever.

The sound of the flight attendant clearing her throat brought Tracie back to reality. Her cheeks heated and she moved back from Rip.

"Sorry to interrupt, but you two need to buckle up. We'll be landing shortly."

Fumbling with her seat belt, Tracie refused to look into Rip's face, afraid of what she'd see. He wanted an answer, but she wasn't ready to give him one. She was afraid that if she put him off too long, he'd quit asking, yet she was more afraid to accept his offer, commit her heart and have it crushed again.

The plane banked to the left and circled a small airport in the Virginia countryside. When the craft came to a complete stop, Tracie unbuckled her seat belt and stood, stretching.

Rip did the same, wincing when he moved his injured arm. His gaze connected with hers. "Ready?"

"Ready." She led the way down the gangway to the ground where a limousine stood. With a deep breath and she stepped into the limo and slid over for Rip to climb in next to her.

"Where to first?" Tracie asked Rip.

The chauffeur, his hand pausing in the process of closing the door, answered, "Mr. Derringer suggested I take you shopping for appropriate attire at, as he put it, a high-end establishment. He has made arrangements for you two to meet with Vance Tate at Blackburn Manufacturing at four o'clock this afternoon."

Tracie nodded. If they were going in as an insanely affluent couple, they need to look the part. Nothing like a little shopping therapy to calm the nerves.

RIP HELPED TRACIE out of the limousine at the entrance to the Blackburn Gun Manufacturing building in Alexandria, Virginia. The large building stood in an industrial park surrounded by similar buildings.

Tracie stretched one silky, sexy leg out of the limo, followed by the other and stood, smoothing the slim-fitting, simple, black designer dress she'd purchased for the occasion. It hugged every inch of her body and the neckline dipped low, displaying an ample amount of her breasts. Accessorized with a simple diamond drop necklace and earrings, a large designer handbag and Jimmy Choo black stilettos, Tracie was stunning.

When she'd walked out of the dress shop wearing the complete ensemble, Rip had to swallow several times before he could comment. Now, all he wanted to do was take her somewhere private and strip the damned dress off and make love to her.

He'd chosen a gray suit and black button-down shirt beneath the jacket, leaving it opened several buttons and wearing no tie. Hank had insisted on a Rolex watch and designer shoes to complete the disguise.

"Mrs. Gideon, shall we?" He settled a hand in the small of her back and guided her toward the front entrance.

Vance Tate met them at the door, wearing a charcoal-gray suit, white shirt and red power tie. He held the door open as Rip and Tracie strode through. "Welcome, Mr. and Mrs. Gideon. So glad you could make it to tour the factory."

"It was nice of you to make time for us on such short notice. Mr. Tate, was it?" Tracie said.

Tate held out his hand. "Vance Tate."

She ignored his outstretched hand and continued. "Chuck and I are only in town for a few hours and we have dinner plans with friends in DC."

Rip took the man's hand and shook it. "Nice to meet you, Mr. Tate."

"Please, call me Vance." The man gestured toward a door on the other side of the lobby entrance. "If you'll come into our conference room, I can show you what we manufacture here at Blackburn."

Rip held up a hand. "We've done our homework and we know *what* you make. We'd like to see your facilities to ensure that you don't skimp on the materials used to manufacture the weapons we're interested in purchasing."

"We use only the best materials," Vance assured him. "I can show you around the factory, then we can sit and discuss your needs."

"Very well." Rip crossed his arms, hoping to convey to the man that he was waiting to be impressed.

Vance led the way past a reception desk, slid his identification badge through a card reader and held the door for Tracie and Rip. "Your secretary gave us an idea of what you were looking for, but perhaps you could elaborate?"

"As my secretary was to inform you, the weapons we require are to provide security to our villa in Costa Rica. I do not intend to take my wife there until the security personnel and their weapons are in place." Rip slipped his arm around Tracie's waist and pulled her against him. "I will spare no expense to keep my wife safe. She is my most important possession."

Anticipating her elbow jab to his gut, his muscles were tight, ready to take the blow, knowing she'd take offense to being called a possession. Rip could barely contain his smile.

Vance handed them safety glasses and ear protection headsets. He led them through the different buildings of the manufacturing facility. They started in an area where materials and spare parts were received, their certification documents scanned and filed. From there, they entered a large room filled with machines that cut away the metal to shape the outside of the barrels and rifled the insides. In a clean room, several workers along a line assembled the parts by hand.

Tate entered a long hallway with doors along the length, walking past several without stopping.

"What's behind these doors?" Tracie asked.

"Offices and storerooms." Vance passed the restrooms and took them to the end of the hallway. "I think you will find this interesting." He pushed through a door into another building. "We have an indoor range where each weapon is tested with live rounds. If you'd like, you could fire one of the weapons you're interest in purchasing." He reached for a rifle hanging on a rack along the wall. When he turned to face the two of them, Tracie stepped forward and held out her hands. "I'd like that."

Vance's brows rose as he handed the weapon over. "A gun enthusiast?"

Rip smiled over Tracie's head. "My wife is a woman of many talents. I assure you, she's an expert shot. All those skeet-shooting lessons paid off. Right, sweetheart?" He kissed her temple. "This rifle is similar to the M4A1, is it not?"

Vance nodded, his brow furrowed. "Yes, sir."

Rip looked down at Tracie, "While you get set up, I'd like to retrieve my hearing protection headset I left in the car." He grimaced and pointed to his ears. "The doctor warned me that I could lose what's left of my hearing if I don't take care."

"I'll need to go with you." Vance glanced from Rip to Tracie and back to Rip, his frown deepening. "Visitors aren't allowed to be in the factory without an escort."

"I'll be all right. I know the way back. It's not as though I'd be wandering through the manufacturing areas."

Tracie lifted the weapon to her shoulder and stared down the site. "Do you have a clip and bullets, Mr. Tate?" she asked.

Vance hesitated for a moment. "I guess it will be okay if you go straight there and return directly. And yes, I can get those bullets for you." The salesman turned to help Tracie.

Rip took the opportunity to slip out of the range building and back into the hallway. He opened several doors belonging to offices. One was empty with Vance's name plate on the desk inside. Another had a woman seated at a desk piled high with paperwork. "May I help you?" she asked, barely looking up.

"Just looking for the restroom," Rip said with his most charming smile.

The woman's eyes and her harried expression softened. "Down the hall on the left."

"Thank you." Rip ducked out and moved to the next door. It was locked. Using a slim metal file, he slipped it into the keyhole and turned it, triggering the locking mechanism. When he twisted the door handle the door opened.

The room was too dark to see very far inside. Pulling a small flashlight from his pocket, he switched it on to reveal a much larger work area, with an overhead door at the far side. Crates lined up along the floors and were stacked against the walls. Inside the crates were more parts to be used in the assembly of the weapons. In the ceiling corners of the large room were cameras, the green blinking lights indicating they were active. Someone at the other end of the cable was monitoring this room.

Rip checked the hallway behind him—*clear*—and stepped inside, closing and locking the door behind him. Without the overhead lights shining down on him, the video cameras wouldn't be able to make out his face.

Making a quick turn around the room, using a red filter on his flashlight and creating a barrier between the light and the security cameras with his body, he checked the contents of several boxes. Nowhere did he find anything resembling M4A1s.

When he'd run out of time, he stopped at the door and listened before opening it a crack and peering out into the hallway. The click, click, click of a lady's high heels alerted him to someone coming down the hallway.

Closing the door, he twisted the lock just as the heels stopped clicking directly in front of the door.

Rip held his breath and inched to the side of the door, resting his hand lightly on the knob. If someone opened it, he'd be hidden temporarily behind the door. But not for long. If the woman turned on the lights, entered and shut the door behind her, he'd be exposed.

The cool metal knob beneath his fingers shifted slightly. The lock held and the knob stopped moving. The knob turned slightly again. A moment later the heels tapped against the tile floor of the hallway and the sound diminished, leaving silence in its wake.

Knowing Vance would come looking for him soon, Rip edged the door open. The hallway was clear. Leaving the room, he locked the door behind him and returned the way he'd come, pausing at the door to Vance's office.

He opened it, peered inside and almost left before he spotted a door nearly hidden by a file cabinet. After glancing over his shoulder, he slipped into the office, noting a distinct lack of cameras here.

The possibility of finding a key was slim—if there were something worth hiding in the room beyond, the key would not be in the man's desk, it would be on him. Rip stuck the metal file he'd used on the other door into the keyhole and jiggled the lock. It wasn't budging.

He tried the file in the keyhole again and this time, the lock released.

Rip pushed through the door. As he suspected, the door led into a large storage room and workspace. He checked the upper corners of the room for cameras. Finding none, he flipped the light switch and illuminated the dark room. Near the end of the row, he located four large crates marked Spare Parts. The lids were nailed shut.

Quickly locating a crowbar from a long workbench on the wall, Rip levered the nails loose and pushed the lid aside. Brown paper covered the top. Below were brand-new M4A1 military-issue rifles complete with serial numbers and the manufacturers logo engraved on the manufacturing identification plate.

A bill of lading indicated this shipment had been meant to go to a US Army warehouse at Fort Lee, Virginia. Nothing on the outside of the box indicated the destination. In fact, there was no writing on the outside of the box. Whatever shipping documents had been originally attached to the box had been removed.

Rip snapped photos of the weapons with his cell phone.

His chest squeezed. He'd found the source of the modified M4A1 rifles and Vance Tate was knee deep in the operation.

The big question was who had diverted the shipment of military weapons to Blackburn Gun Manufacturing? Whoever it was had some connection to military procurement somewhere along the supply chain. Vance was his only link to the misappropriated weapons, and he was with Tracie. How desperate would he be if he knew his illegal arms trade had been discovered?

His gut clenching, Rip set the box lids in place, left the room and turned out the light. The sooner he got back to Tracie the better.

Once he made it to Vance's office, his cell phone vibrated in his back pocket. He whipped out the phone and read the text message from Hector on the screen, his heartbeat skidding to a stop.

Delgado escaped. My sources say he boarded a plane for the US.

Even if Delgado hadn't boarded a plane for the States, he would still notify his supplier that he'd been captured and the weapons' supply chain had been compromised. Any minute now, Vance Tate would get the word.

Rip and Tracie had to get out. *Now.*

# *Chapter Sixteen*

Tracie knew she had to keep Vance Tate distracted long enough for Rip to search the immediate premises for any sign of illegal arms trade.

"I suppose you're an expert shot, are you not, Mr. Tate?"

"I am. I have the weapons and the range to practice as much as I want. I wouldn't be a good salesman if didn't familiarize myself with the weapons I'm selling in order to provide the best information to my customers."

"You're a very good salesman, Mr. Tate." Tracie lined up her sites and pulled the trigger, hitting the target dead center of the silhouette's heart.

"Nice shot, Mrs. Gideon." Vance stood beside her, one earpiece of his headset pulled off his ear. "Do you mind if I call you Phyllis?"

She shrugged and lined up her sights again. "I don't mind. But my husband is a very jealous man." If she were in a relationship with Rip, would he be jealous of other men if they found her attractive? Pulling the trigger, she hit the target just barely off the original bullet hole.

"How many semiautomatic rifles are you interested in ordering for you security guards?" Vance asked.

Without hesitating, she answered, "At least fifty."

A beep sounded from Vance's breast pocket and he

dug out a cell phone, as he stated, "That's a lot of guns for a villa."

"I intend to hire fifty guards. I want each of my guards to have his own weapon in case of an emergency or uprising."

Vance's lips twisted. "I thought Costa Rica was pretty stable at this time."

Tracie raised her brows and gave Vance what she hoped was a questioning, yet sexy look, not that she was used to playing the sex-kitten wife of a billionaire. "You of all people know that no Central American country is completely stable. Where there are desperately poor people, there are thieves and opportunists."

Vance held the cell phone without looking down at the screen, a slight frown making lines across his forehead. "If you're not comfortable with the location, why buy a villa there?"

Tracie finished off the rounds in the clip, nailing the target with one after the other. When the clip was empty, she released it and handed it to Vance, her hand lingering in his. "Where else can I go where I can make the rules?" She faced him, a smile curling her lips. "If I feel like it, I can sunbathe in the nude and make love to my husband in broad daylight without being thrown in jail for indecent exposure."

Vance's eyes flared and his attention drifted to the V-neckline of her little black dress. He swallowed, Adam's apple bobbing as he handed her another clip. "I suppose of all the countries in Central America, Cost Rica is the least dangerous. And if you have the money to hire your own army, you can live anywhere you want."

"Precisely." Tracie shoved the clip into the rifle, lifted the rifle to her shoulder again and aimed. "I like things a certain way, and I get what I want." She fired the weapon and turned to glance at Vance.

His gaze had shifted to the cell phone in his hand.

From the corner of her eye, Tracie saw the man stiffen, his jaw tightening, his fingers curling around the device. "Mrs. Gideon, did you say you and your husband were only in town for a couple of days?"

Her pulse kicking up a notch, Tracie feigned a calm she didn't feel as she answered. "That's right. We have dinner with friends in DC later tonight."

"Where did you fly in from?"

Still holding the rifle, she faced Vance, unwaveringly. "Dallas, why?"

Vance held a nine-millimeter Glock in his hand, pointed at her gut. "I don't think so." In his other hand, he held up his cell phone and showed her a picture of her and Rip, standing outside Delgado's house on *le Plantación de Ángel.*

Her heart plummeted to the pit of her belly.

"How interesting that you have a picture of my husband and me on our vacation to Honduras." Tracie leaned toward Vance and frowned. "I'm appalled at the arrogance of the paparazzi." She waved her hand at the weapon in his hand. "Am I firing that one next?" she asked, reaching out to take the handgun from him.

Vance jerked his hand back. "Hell no. What you're going to do is tell me why you were in Honduras in the first place."

"My dear, Mr. Tate. We take vacations in a variety of locations. Honduras just happens to be one of them."

Vance shook his head. "Save your lies for some dumb schmuck who'll believe them. I suspect you and Mr. Gideon, if those are even your real names, are casing my factory."

"Should we be? Only men with something to hide would be concerned about being played for a fool."

"Doesn't matter. My boss knows what went down in

Honduras and he's mad as hell. Guess you and I will be paying him a visit." Vance snatched at her arm.

Tracie slammed the rifle she'd been carrying into Vance's chest, knocking his handgun from his grip. She dodged him and made a run for the door, her slim-fitting skirt hampering her stride.

He caught her before she reached it, wrapped his arms around her middle, clamping her arms to her sides. Vance held on as she kicked, bucked and fought to throw him off.

Tracie had to warn Rip that they'd been discovered. If she didn't, he could be walking right into a trap. Gathering all her strength, she planted her feet on the ground, hunched over and nearly tossed Vance over her back.

He lost his balance for a moment, then dug his heels into the ground and lifted her off her feet, carrying her toward a door on the far side of the range, opposite the one Rip had disappeared through what seemed like such a long time before.

The door he carried her through led to another short hallway with an exit. As they neared, he fought to free one of his hands.

Now would be the time to make her break for it.

Tracie braced her feet against the door and shoved backward, knocking Vance onto his backside.

He hit with such force, his arms loosened momentarily. Just long enough for Tracie to roll to the side and spring to her feet.

Two steps brought her to the door. She twisted the knob, threw it open and ran outside and straight into the arms of one of Vance's oversize henchmen.

He crushed her to his chest and squeezed until she thought every one of her bones would snap beneath the pressure. She couldn't breathe and she couldn't move.

A cloth was shoved over her nose.

Desperate to breathe, Tracie inhaled, a biting scent stinging her nostrils. Her world went black.

RIP BURST THROUGH the doorway leading to the indoor range. The absolute silence struck him first. No voices, no pop or bang of rounds being fired.

His heart plummeted as he ran to the spot where he'd left Tracie. On the floor lay the rifle she'd held when he'd excused himself to go to the restroom.

He hadn't passed anyone in the hallway, nor had he heard a scuffle. Vance and Tracie had to have taken an alternate exit from the range. After a quick scan of the range facility, he spotted a doorway on the opposite end of the firing stations. Rip grabbed the rifle Tracie had been firing from the floor and ran for the door and flung it open. A short, empty hallway led to yet another doorway. By the time he reached it, he already knew what he'd find.

He opened it and stared out onto an empty parking lot. Tracie was gone. Rip knew in his gut, Vance had taken her. How had he walked away without planting a tracking device on her?

Her cell phone. If she'd managed to keep it, they had a way of tracking her.

Rip pulled his mobile phone from his pocket and dialed Hank's number.

He answered on the first ring. "Rip, what did you find out at the Blackburn factory?"

"I found the room where they grind the serial numbers and logos off the M4A1s. But that's not why I'm calling."

"What's wrong?" Hank asked.

"Vance Tate has Tracie."

"Where?"

"I don't know. I need you to locate her cell phone. If she still has it on her, we have a chance of finding her."

Hank's voice faded out as he gave orders to someone in the same room with him. Then he was back on the line. "I have men on the ground in DC. They've been on alert since you and Tracie landed."

"They won't do me any good if we don't find Tracie."

"Brandon is bringing up the tracking device on her cell phone. It's moving."

Rip let go of the breath he'd been holding. "Which way?" Rather than waste his time searching the factory, he ran back to the room with the guns, took one of the originals and one of the modified weapons, stuffed them into a gym bag he found in Vance's office and ran back to the entrance where he'd met Vance.

A security guard stepped in front of him. "I'm sorry, but I have to search all bags leaving the premises."

"Like hell you do." Rip jerked the bag up, clipping the guard in the chin. The man staggered backward and fell to the floor. The woman behind the reception counter screamed and ducked below her desk, probably dialing 911 as Rip raced for the door.

He didn't give a damn. Vance had Tracie. If he was scared enough, he might try to kill her.

The limousine that had dropped them off pulled up to the curb. The passenger window already down, the driver yelled, "Get in!"

Rip dove into the passenger seat and slammed the door.

The driver hit the accelerator so hard, the rear of the long limousine skidded on the pavement, burning rubber.

Rip was thrown against the door he'd just closed. When the vehicle straightened, Rip did, too, and buckled his seat belt.

"Here, hold this." The driver shoved his cell phone into Rip's hands. "Tell me which way to turn while I drive."

"Rip?" Hank's voice shouted into the headset.

"Yeah, Hank. It's me. Which way?"

Hank guided them through the streets and onto an expressway.

"It appears as though they're exiting into a rest area. If you hurry, you might catch up with them."

Rip peered through the windshield, willing the limo to go faster. The flash of a blue information sign caught his attention and his heart beat faster. The sign indicated a rest area in one mile. "Take the exit for the rest area."

Leaning forward, Rip couldn't get closer to the windshield without bumping his forehead. "Are they moving?"

"No," Hank said.

Hope swelled in Rip's chest as they barreled down the exit ramp into the rest area.

"We're here," Rip said, staring into every car parked along the curbs. One held a heavyset man, his equally heavyset wife and children. A man in jeans and a T-shirt climbed into a pickup and backed out of a space.

The limo driver pulled along the curb taking up several spaces while Rip hopped out and ran along the line of cars, clutching the phone to his ear. He didn't find Tate or Tracie. "Are you sure they're still here?"

"Yes, the tracker says the phone is there."

His hope fading, Rip came to a stop in front of the brick bathroom buildings. "Hank, call Tracie."

"Calling," he responded.

A moment later, Rip heard a cell phone ring. He followed the sound to a trash receptacle, dug down inside and found the new handbag Tracie had bought for the tour through Blackburn. Inside was the cell phone Tracie had carried with her since she'd found him in Biloxi.

Lifting Tracie's phone to his ear, he pressed the talk button, his gut clenched. "She's gone. Her cell phone was dumped."

"Damn." Hank said something to whoever was in the room with him. "Sorry, Rip. I have Brandon backtracking through Belinda's phone numbers to find Vince Tate's personal cell phone. As soon as we have anything, I'll call."

Rip stood on the sidewalk in the rest area and stared around. He had nothing to go on, nowhere to look and had never felt more helpless in his life. Instead of shouting his frustration, he climbed into the limousine.

"Where to?" the driver said.

The only answer he could think of was, "DC."

As the driver shifted into gear, the cell phone in Rip's hand beeped and a message flashed onto the screen.

If you want to see her alive, meet me at the Lion Shipyard in Norfolk, pier 10 at midnight. Bring 5 million dollars. Come alone.

"Change of plan." Rip turned to the driver. "We're headed for Norfolk."

Rip contacted Hank and relayed the demands.

"I'll have the money brought to you by ten o'clock tonight, along with my best men."

"I have to go in alone."

"I understand. But that doesn't mean you won't have backup. Get to Norfolk. The money will be there by ten."

Rip settled back in the passenger seat of the limousine and watched as they passed rural farmland, cities and traffic congestion.

"My name's Ben Harding." The driver stuck out his hand.

Rip looked over at the man and took his hand. Ben's grip was firm and he nodded.

"So are you one of Hank's men?"

"Yeah, I was one of the original Covert Cowboys."

"You know Tracie?"

"Not really. I've been away on assignment. We've met in passing, but I haven't gotten to know her, although Kosart's reputation as an FBI special agent was solid. It got her on as the first female Covert Cowboy. I think she was ready to leave the FBI after her fiancé and the regional director double-crossed her. She almost died in the hands of the Mexican mafia."

"She's tough." *And beautiful, and has a heart of gold.* Rip would give anything to have her back and safe.

"It's hard enough when you're the one being shot at. At least you feel like you have some control. But when it's your partner…" Ben sighed. "I'd tell you not to worry, she can handle herself, but that won't do any good if she's outnumbered."

Rip's fingers clenched into a fist. If they hurt her…

Ben continued, "I will tell you, though, Hank is a good man. If there's a way out of this, he'll throw everything he owns at it to see that Kosart comes home safely. He's done it before. He's the one who sent the Covert Cowboys in to rescue her from the mafia. He didn't give up on her then, he sure as hell won't give up on her now that she works for him."

"That's nice to know." As they neared the outskirts of Norfolk, Rip had Ben take him to the airport where he rented a nondescript two-door sedan that looked like anything else on the streets.

On Hank's orders, Ben rented an SUV. In the separate vehicles, they drove farther out to a smaller, local airport and waited. The sun set around eight, which gave them two full hours to kill until Hank's plane would arrive with the money.

Rip leaned back in his vehicle and closed his eyes. Before each mission he'd performed with the Navy SEALs he'd force himself to relax, to let his body gather the strength he'd need to face the enemy. Each time he had known his skills and awareness were what stood between the enemy and his team. If he wasn't at his best, he was letting his team down.

With Tracie's life on the line, he had a harder time relaxing. Every sound made him jump and his body twitched with the need to take action. There was no way he'd relax until he had her back in his arms. His gunshot wound didn't help with the tension, but he ignored the pain, pushing it aside for now.

A few minutes before ten, the blinking lights of an incoming aircraft brought Rip out of the car and onto his feet.

The Citation X landed on the tarmac and pulled to a stop. When the stairs were lowered, a man in peak condition but with a shock of white hair stepped out of the plane and settled a cowboy hat on his head. Rip knew that face from the video feeds on board the Citation.

Ben joined Rip as they strode through the hangar and out onto the tarmac. "You haven't met Hank, have you?"

"Not in person." Rip stepped forward. "Mr. Derringer, I'm Cord Schafer. Folks call me Rip."

Hank's grip was firm. "Would rather have met you under better circumstances, but that's not important. What is important is getting Ms. Kosart back alive."

"I like the way you think."

Hank turned to the plane gangway and nodded at the man standing at the top with a suitcase in his hand. The man was big like a linebacker, making the door to the plane seem too small for his broad shoulders. He turned sideways and descended the steps.

Two more men followed him out of the plane.

"Rip, meet Chuck Bolton." Hank indicated the man with the suitcase.

Chuck held out a hand and shook Rip's, practically crushing his fingers.

"Zachary Adams and Thorn Drennan will also be joining the team," Hank said.

Zachary and Thorn both shook hands with Rip and then smiled and shook hands with Ben.

"Good to see you, Harding," Adams said.

Ben turned to Chuck. "I hear you're expecting another kid. Congrats."

Chuck nodded, a grin spreading across his face. "Didn't know being a dad was going to be so much work and so rewarding."

Rip didn't have time for pleasantries.

Adams turned to Rip, his jaw tight, his brows furrowed. "Just so you know, I have a stake in this rescue operation. Tracie Kosart is my fiancée's twin. If I don't come back with good news, I've been told not to come back."

Adam's words hit Rip in the chest. He hadn't known Tracie had a twin. Hell, he didn't know much about her at all. But damn it, *he would*. Once this thing was over, he would make Tracie see reason and go out with him. Then he'd ask all those questions they hadn't had time for since they'd met.

"We will get Ms. Kosart back," Hank said. "There's no *if* about it." He motioned Chuck forward and had him set the case on the ground. Then he bent to flick the catches open and stood back for the men to see inside.

Adams, Bolton, Harding and Drennan whistled, as impressed by the amount of cash packed into the case as Rip was.

"That's a lot of money to be carrying around," Thorn said, his tone deep, resonant.

"A man could get killed carrying around such a stash." Ben's voice filled the darkness.

"That's why I brought along a security detail." Hank crossed his arms. "Though you'll be going in alone, my men will infiltrate the shipyard ahead of you and be there for you."

Rip shook his head. "I don't know. If they get wind of any of you, it could jeopardize Tracie's safety."

"My men are highly skilled, each coming to me with excellent records in their prior lives and positions."

Rip's lips thinned. "Are you willing to bet Tracie's life on them?"

"I'm counting on them to help you get Tracie back alive." Hank's eyes narrowed. "I value each and every member of my team and the people we swear to defend and protect. I won't let the men who've taken her hurt her. I give you my word."

For a long moment Rip stared into Hank's eyes. The man appeared sincere and committed to getting Tracie back. "If that's the case, we need to be going. I'm due to meet with them at midnight."

Bolton, Harding, Adams and Drennan helped offload an astonishing array of weapons from the plane into the SUV and then climbed in.

Hank stood beside Rip. "You need to arm yourself."

"I have a .40 caliber strapped around my calf and a nine-millimeter Glock under my shirt. Anything more than that and they'll see it. I'm risking enough as it is. The idea is to give them the money and get Tracie out of there. If you and your men want to go after them, that's fine. I'll help as long as we get Tracie clear first."

"I agree." Hank touched a hand to Rip's arm. "We'll get her back." The older man extended his hand and Rip shook it. When Hank withdrew his hand, he left what appeared to be a coin in Rip's palm. "I want you to have this."

"What is it?" Rip turned the coin over. It looked like

one of the gold-colored dollar coins he occasionally got for change from a soda machine.

"My good-luck charm. Although, for the most part, I believe in making my own luck. But it doesn't hurt to carry some with you."

Rip shrugged and stuffed the coin in his pocket. "Thanks. I'm not supposed to be there until midnight. You and your men have until then to get into place."

Hank climbed into the SUV with the other four operatives and they set off.

A glance at his watch made his stomach clench. One hour until he was to meet the men who held Tracie captive. For the first time in a long time he prayed. In the few days he'd known her, she'd come to mean more to him than any other woman he'd ever met. Never one to believe in love at first sight, he could be well on his way there with Hank's only female Covert Cowboy.

As he climbed into the little sedan, he thought back over all he and Tracie had been through together. No other woman he knew would have handled it as well. She was tough, but sensitive, passionate and gentle.

When he got her back, he'd insist they go out on a real date before he had to go back to Mississippi, and she headed back to Texas or wherever Hank chose to send her. Somehow he'd convince her that they should continue seeing each other.

The drive to Lion Shipyard took thirty minutes. For the next twenty, he parked in an empty parking lot outside the fenced-in compound, waited and prayed.

## Chapter Seventeen

Tracie woke in a very dark, cramped place that smelled of old tires and gasoline. An engine rumbled, making her tomb vibrate. Based on the noise, darkness and movement beneath her, she was locked in the trunk of a car. The metal hood and walls of the vehicle seemed to close in around her. Her heart raced and her breaths came in short, spiky gasps. She had to calm herself or she'd pass out again.

Taking deep breaths of the smelly air, she forced herself to think of a way out of the vehicle. The backseats of many sedans were equipped with a fold-down seat to carry a long load from the trunk into the cab of the car.

Running her hands along the seam of the trunk lid, she searched for the emergency release lever. Her fingers encountered a ragged piece of metal she guessed was the broken lever. She redirected her search to the back of the seat, hoping to find a lever to release the locks holding the seat in place. If she could get through the backseat without being detected, she could somehow take out the driver and the passenger and make her escape. She found nothing but the hard back of the seat. What she needed was a weapon. The dress she'd worn had been so tight, hiding a gun or knife beneath it hadn't been an option, and they'd ditched her purse somewhere along the way. Tracie felt around the trunk, finding nothing but the shoes she'd been wearing and a hard metal tab.

Her heart thumped in her chest. Most new cars stored the spare tire beneath a panel in the trunk. The tab had to be there to allow access to the tools needed to change a tire, like a jack, the crank and a heavy wrench to loosen the lug nuts.

Tracie tried to roll to one side and out of the way so that she could get to the tools before the vehicle came to a stop. If she didn't have some way to defend herself, she could be dragged out on the ground and dispatched with a bullet in the back of her head.

She'd sworn she'd never allow herself to be kidnapped ever again. Not after Mexico. Yet here she was, captive in the trunk of a car heading who knew where. Her only hope was that Rip would be tearing up heaven and earth to find her.

She laughed, the sound choked by a sob. If only she could get the cover off the storage compartment, she might find a lug wrench or something heavy to hit her captors with and distract them long enough to get away. If Rip found her, she didn't want him to walk into a trap.

The SEAL had grown on her and she wanted to see him again. Preferably under better circumstances. She'd been toying with the idea and now knew, if she didn't die that night, she wanted to go out on that date with her "husband."

Her lips curled at the irony of the situation. They were married before they'd had a first date. Okay, so the marriage had never taken place, but they'd done a helluva job pretending to be a married couple, and they had more in common than most married couples she knew.

They both loved a good firearm. They were both in dangerous lines of business, and they both wanted to live in a cabin in the mountains. Those few things she knew about him only made her want to know so much more. Like which was his favorite football team, could he ride a horse and did he have any living family members?

Thinking of family, Tracie wished she could get word to her sister. And tell her what? *I'm alive for the moment, but all bets are off when the car stops.*

The car made a turn, rolling her to the side. With her hand on the tab, the cover came up with her and she shoved it aside.

Patting the well beneath her she felt around for the familiar hard steel of a lug wrench. A small temporary doughnut tire lay in the middle of the well. Beside it was what felt like a jack stand. She couldn't find a tire iron or lug wrench.

*Damn.* What idiot drove a vehicle without the proper emergency equipment? She almost laughed hysterically at her thought, then sobered as the car slowed to a stop.

Fumbling to remove the jack stand from where it was screwed into the bottom of the well, she found a wing nut and twisted it loose as fast as she could. When she had it out, she set it aside.

The engine cut off and doors opened and closed.

Moving as quietly as she could, she slid the lid over the well and rolled over it. She pushed the jack stand behind her, hiding it and her hand from view.

When her captors opened the trunk, they'd be in for a big surprise.

The lock on the trunk popped and the lid rose, letting in only a small amount of light.

Tracie kept her eyes closed most of the way, peeking through the slits. When a man bent over and grabbed her arm, she launched herself at him, swinging her other hand with the jack stand in it at her attacker's head. It hit with a dull thump.

The man's grip loosened and he crumpled to the ground with a groan.

Tracie scrambled out of the trunk, falling to the ground beside the man she'd hit. Before she could scramble to her feet, the big man who'd captured her outside Blackburn grabbed her around the middle and held on.

She fought, kicking and biting until he slammed a fist into her face, hitting her cheek so hard, her head jerked back and everything faded to gray. She tried to hang on, willing her eyes to stay focused.

In the meantime, Vance Tate rose to his feet and backhanded her. "Bitch! I oughta kill you for that." Blood oozed from a gash on Tate's temple and he wiped it away with the back of his sleeve.

Dizzy, her knees threatening to buckle, Tracie's head swayed in the dark searching for another escape plan. From what she could tell, they were in a dark alley between brick warehouses that were completely dark. Even if she screamed, she doubted anyone would hear her.

Headlights illuminated the darkness. A vehicle sped toward them. For a moment Tracie thought it wasn't going to stop, would run them over.

At the last minute, the vehicle, a black SUV, screeched to a halt, kicking up gravel and dust in their faces.

A man wearing a suit and a dark fedora stepped out of the vehicle, the hat pulled down over his forehead, hiding his eyes from them. "What's the meaning of this?" the man growled. "Why is she here?"

Vance jerked a thumb toward her. "This woman and her husband came to Blackburn today asking about purchasing guns."

The man crossed his arms over his chest. "So?"

"They are the ones Delgado told us about. He's mad as

hell and is on his way here. He thinks this woman and her husband are responsible for destroying his entire camp."

"What does that have to do with me? You know I don't get involved in the details."

"If this woman and her husband are responsible, as Delgado says they are, we could be in big trouble. I want out. I don't even know if she was involved, but it was too much of a coincidence."

"Where's the husband?" Fedora demanded.

"I don't know. When I heard Delgado was on his way here, I left with the woman and called you immediately."

"Look," Tracie said, struggling against the arms locked around her middle. "I have no idea what you're talking about. This is just a big mistake. If you let me go, I'll walk away, no harm, no foul."

"Shut up!" Vance popped the side of her head with a forceful slap.

Tracie tried to break free of the big man's hold, but he was stronger and refused to release her.

"It's too late," Fedora said. "She already knows more than she should."

"What do I know?" Tracie argued. "I came to buy guns for my vacation home in Costa Rica. I don't know what you two are talking about or who this Delgado guy is. Just let me go. My husband will be worried sick."

As if she hadn't said a word, Fedora focused on Vance. "You know my policy."

Vance's entire body shook. "Yes, sir, but—"

The mystery man held up his hand. "You've compromised my cover."

"I had to. They know."

"Know what? Really." Tracie shook her head. "I have no idea what you're talking about. I just want to go home, kick up my feet and drink a very dry martini. Maybe two."

Fedora man didn't move a muscle. In a voice that sent chills up and down Tracie's spine, he said, "Kill her."

"Whoa, wait a minute," Tracie said. "This is one big ugly mistake. If it's all the same to you, I'll buy my guns somewhere else."

Vance backed up a step. "I'm not doing your dirty work for you. This is Delgado's mess. Other than a grainy photo and Delgado's text, I'm not even certain they did anything wrong."

"We can settle that right now." Fedora raised his hand and motioned for someone to join them. The passenger door of the SUV opened and a man dropped to the ground.

At first all Tracie could see was his silhouette. When he passed beside the headlights, she caught a glimpse of his face.

Carmelo Delgado.

Tracie's blood ran cold and she leaned her head forward, letting her hair fall partially over her face, praying the man didn't recognize her for the woman who had come to ask about his coffee plantation.

"Is this the woman?" Fedora asked.

Delgado walked straight up to her, grabbed a handful of hair and yanked it back, exposing her face to the headlights.

*"Si."* He cursed in Spanish and then backhanded her so hard, she almost fell. If not for the big guy's arm around her middle, she would have been knocked to the ground.

Her jaw and cheek ached and the tissue around her right eye began to swell.

"Kill her," Fedora demanded.

Delgado's eyes narrowed and he pulled his fist back to hit her again.

"Wait." Vance held up a hand. "You can't kill her. Her husband is still running around out there. I've arranged for him to meet me at Lion's Shipyard at midnight. He'll want proof she's alive before he reveals himself to us."

Delgado looked to Fedora.

For a long moment, Fedora paused. "How did you get him to agree to come?"

"I told him to bring five million dollars in cash in exchange for his wife."

"Where exactly are you meeting him?" Fedora straightened the sleeve of his suit jacket, appearing to be in no hurry.

Warning bells went off in Tracie's head. The man was like a snake, quietly tensing to strike.

"At Lion's Shipyard, pier ten." Vance added, "At midnight."

"How did you arrange this?"

Vance pulled a cell phone out of his pocket. "I used this disposable phone. I signed up for it using a fake name."

"Clever," Fedora said. "Let me see that." He held out his hand.

Vance placed the phone in the man's hand.

In the next second, the world exploded around Tracie, and Vance fell. Knocking into the man holding her and taking them both down.

Another gunshot made the big guy jerk and then his arm loosened.

Slightly dazed, Tracie fought to free herself from the tangle of bodies.

Delgado yanked her up by the hair, jerked her hands behind her back and secured them with a zip tie. He tossed her over his shoulder and carried her to the back of the SUV and dumped her inside.

Her night wasn't going very well at all, but Vance and his bouncer friend's had ended even worse.

Tracie vowed to live long enough to return Delgado's

favor and slug him in the face. Then she'd figure a way out of the mess she was in and expose the man in the Fedora. He seemed to have the power, and she planned to bring him down.

AT TEN MINUTES to midnight, Rip found a gap beneath the fence and slid the suitcase full of money under the chain link, then he dropped to the ground and rolled beneath the wire. Once inside he patted the gun in the holster under his shirt. It was little reassurance against an enemy he didn't know much about. All he knew was that Vance had taken Tracie. How many more men would show up to protect his investment was a mystery.

He walked between tall stacks of huge metal containers, aiming for the end of the dock where pier ten was located. Right at midnight he arrived and waited in the shadows of the containers, craning his neck to see beyond, hoping to catch a glimpse of Tracie. Nothing moved. He didn't know whether or not Hank's team was in place.

At three minutes past twelve, his cell phone rang.

He fumbled in his pocket for the device and answered.

"There is a forklift three rows from where you are standing. Get in it and drive it down to pier number six. Leave your cell phone where you're standing. If anyone follows you, the girl is dead. You have exactly two minutes to get there. If you aren't there by then, the girl dies. Now go!"

"I want to hear her voice. Prove to me she's alive," he demanded. His demand was greeted with the silence of the call having ended. With less than a minute to spare, he dropped his phone, ran two aisles of containers over and found the forklift with the key still in it. Rip pushed the lever toward the front of the device and the forklift shot forward. Manipulating the many levers, he finally got the forklift heading in the right direction, having wasted too much time already.

He raced past several piers, counting backward from Pier ten to the sixth one. He would have to handle the exchange alone. If the others moved closer to pier six, they would be seen and risk tipping off Tracie's kidnappers. The money didn't mean anything to him. Tracie did.

Hopefully, with the amount of money they'd demanded, her captors wouldn't feel the need to kill her. Then again, they'd killed the DEA agent to keep their secret. Rip figured there was little chance they'd take the money and leave the girl. Alive.

As he pulled to a halt in front of pier six, he remained in the forklift, hunkered low, using the heavy-duty frame of the machine to shield himself as best he could. He didn't care if he lived or died, but he had to make sure Tracie was safe. He couldn't do that if he was picked off by a sniper.

Shutting off the forklift's engine, he sat for a moment, waiting for Vance to emerge with Tracie. Poised to throw himself off the forklift, he twitched, ready for action, ready to get this over with.

When no one emerged, Rip couldn't wait any longer. "I have the money. Give me the girl."

Again silence.

"One more minute and I leave, taking the money with me. Fifty-nine, fifty-eight, fifty-seven…"

His countdown made it to fifty before a figure detached itself from the shadow of a container stack. "Are you alone?" A man in a Fedora stood in the open, his face still hidden by the brim of his hat.

"Yes. Where's my wife?"

"Come down from the forklift so that I can see you're not armed."

"Show me my wife."

"She's in a safe place." The man waited with his legs slightly apart, his arms crossed. "Show me the money."

"It's in a safe place."

"Touché." Fedora touched a finger to his hat. "Tell me, why would a man and his wife go all the way to Honduras to buy a coffee plantation and then leave without negotiating?"

"We didn't find one for sale."

"Perhaps you didn't ask nicely enough," Fedora said.

Another man emerged from the shadows, and in his arms, he held Tracie, his hand clamped over her mouth. A shaft of light spilled over the man's face, revealing who it was.

Carmelo Delgado.

Rip's heart lurched. He wanted to drop down off the forklift and run to her. But he couldn't tell whether Fedora had a gun in his hand or not. He couldn't take the chance with Tracie's life hanging in the balance.

Tracie struggled to free herself, but Delgado had a powerful hold on the trained agent and it appeared he had her hands tied behind her back.

Thinking fast, Rip called out, "Tell you what. You send the girl halfway and I'll send the money halfway. She can show you that the case is in fact full of the five million dollars you asked for. When I have my wife safely over here, I'll leave and you can take the case. I won't try to stop you. All I ask is that no harm comes to my wife."

"Bring her." Fedora waved Delgado forward with Tracie.

Using the forklift's bulky frame as cover, Rip slipped out of his seat and dropped to the ground. He took the suitcase full of money from behind the seat of the forklift and held it against his chest.

"You need to untie my wife's hands so that she can open the case."

Fedora and Delgado whispered to each other.

Delgado pulled a switchblade out of his pocket and hit the button, popping it open. Then he cut the tie binding Tracie's wrist, immediately pressing the knife to her throat.

Rip's heart stopped and then raced on.

Fedora shouted, "If you do something stupid, I'll have him kill you and then kill your wife."

"Okay, I'll leave the stupid out. On the count of three, send her over, and I'll send the case." Still using the fork-lift for cover, Rip bent and laid the case on the pavement, slipped the strap holding the small .40 caliber pistol from around his calf and buckled it to the handle of the case. If the strap held, the gun would arrive at the midpoint between him and Tracie's captors. "If you want the money, you have to give me the girl."

"Okay. But if you make one wrong move, I'll kill your wife," Fedora warned. Using Delgado and Tracie as a human shield, he backed toward the SUV and ducked behind the door.

Rip held his breath. They could be walking her back to the SUV to take off and find another place to hide her or leave her body.

When they didn't shove her into the vehicle, Rip remembered to breathe. He'd feel better when she was with him and away from Fedora and Delgado.

"Ready?" Fedora called out.

"Ready," Rip responded. "On the count of three. One… two…three."

Delgado gave Tracie a shove, sending her flying toward the case. He ducked behind the door with Fedora and waited.

Rip shoved the case, gun and all toward Tracie, praying she'd see the gun before the others did.

Surreptitiously pulling his Glock from beneath his shirt,

he waited for the fun to begin. As soon as Tracie started out across the pavement, Rip wanted to run out and throw his body over hers to protect her from being shot.

"I have a gun aimed at Mrs. Gideon," Fedora noted. "One false move and she is dead."

Tracie walked toward the case and bent down beside it. She fumbled with the clasps until they popped open, taking more time than Rip liked.

When he was sure she'd found the gun and had sufficient time to pull it from the holster, he held his breath.

Tracie swiveled on her heels, squatting beside the case, turning it so that they could see inside. "The money is all here."

Rip almost laughed.

Tracie held the gun behind her back, her legs tense, appearing spring-loaded, ready for action. "Coming your way," she said and shoved the case hard enough it went flying at Fedora. Rip had been ready and fired at the same time as Fedora, hitting him square in the chest.

Delgado threw his knife at Tracie.

She dropped to the ground, clutching at the knife in her belly. With a quick jerk, she pulled it out and blood spurted from her body.

Rip fired back at Delgado and lurched toward her, his heart in his throat.

"Look out, Rip!" she yelled.

Fedora sat up and aimed at Rip, but didn't get the chance to pull the trigger.

A shot rang out from somewhere to Rip's right, clipping Fedora in the temple, knocking the hat off his head.

## Chapter Eighteen

Rip reached Tracie and gathered her in his arms, pressing his hand against her wound to slow the blood loss.

"Hey, Mrs. Gideon, you doing all right?" he asked, brushing the hair out of her eyes so that he could see them.

She smiled up at him. "Never better, Mr. Gideon," she answered, her voice weak, her face turning a chalky white.

"Hang in there, we're going to get you fixed up."

"Good. I have a date with my husband I wouldn't want to miss…" Her voice faded and her eyes closed.

Rip's chest squeezed so hard he could barely breathe. "We need an ambulance here!" he yelled.

"Could you keep it down, sweetheart?" Tracie whispered. "A girl needs her beauty sleep."

Keeping his hand pressed to her wound, Rip hugged her close. "That's my girl. You're going to be just fine."

Covert Cowboys surrounded them. Hank brought up the rear, already on the phone calling for assistance. Within minutes, the fire department's emergency vehicle arrived and they loaded Tracie into the ambulance.

Rip couldn't remember a longer trip in his entire life.

Two hours later, he stood in the waiting room, waiting for the surgeon to appear. Hank, Adams, Bolton, Harding and Drennan had gathered around him, awaiting news of Tracie's prognosis.

The entire time they were in the waiting room, Hank had been on and off his cell phone with the authorities, with Rip's commander and with Brandon back at the Raging Bull Ranch.

Hank finally hung up and faced the men. "Brandon verified the identity of the man with Delgado. His name was Mark Kuntz. He's a former soldier from the US Army Special Forces. He was in the same unit as the sniper who tried to kill you several weeks ago, Rip."

Rip's chest felt hollow. "Fenton Rollins?"

"Yes. Brandon found several photographs of the two together in Iraq. And, get this—Kuntz was Senator Thomas Craine's executive assistant."

"Wasn't Craine the one who was working on trade negotiations with several Central American countries?" Rip ran a hand through his hair, sick at the thought of his own countrymen selling them out.

Hank nodded. "I had Brandon search the photographs of Senator Craine's visit to Central America, including the one in which we saw him with Delgado. Mark Kuntz was in that photo, as well. Not prominently featured, but there in the background."

Rip's fists clenched. "Is Senator Craine involved in the illegal arms deals with the terrorists?"

Hank shook his head. "So far, we haven't found a definitive connection other than Kuntz working for Craine. I have Brandon searching every link he can find, digging into their emails, their phone records and their bank accounts. Senator Craine has several corporations he's associated with, some of which have offshore accounts. So far we have nothing and Senator Craine has refused to be interviewed. It's in the Feds' hands now."

Rip drew in a deep breath to calm the rage he felt toward these men who'd become traitors to their own country. "You're not stopping the investigation, are you?"

Hank smiled, though his eyes narrowed. "Not on your life…or Tracie's."

"Good."

"With Mark Kuntz and Fenton Rollins out of the picture now, are you planning to go back to your unit?" Hank asked.

Rip hadn't even gotten past leaving the hospital. He wouldn't leave until he knew for sure Tracie was going to be all right. "I haven't gotten that far."

"When Tracie is released, I'd like you two to take some time off. I'll clear it with your unit commander if you don't mind me arranging things. You need it, and I'm sure Tracie would feel better if you were with her during her recuperation."

Rip glanced at the doorway to the surgical waiting room. "I'm okay with whatever." He didn't care about anything at that moment but getting news from the doctor.

Then a man in scrubs, a hair cap and surgical booties entered the waiting room. "Are you the folks with Tracie Kosart?"

All six of the men answered as one. "Yes."

"Good news. She's going to be just fine. No major damage to internal organs. After a night of observation, she could be ready to go home."

All the air rushed out of Rip's lungs and, for a moment, he felt light-headed. "Can I see her?"

"She's in recovery now and asking for her husband." The doctor's brows rose. "Is that you?"

Rip nearly laughed out loud before he nodded, "That's me." He ran for the door, happier than he'd been since graduating BUD/S.

A WEEK LATER, Tracy lounged in a deck chair, staring out over a mountain valley with a cup of hot cocoa cradled in her hands. "It's just like I imagined it."

"It's better than I had imagined it because you're here." Rip held out his hand, taking one of hers.

"You're a smooth talker, for a frogman." Tracie squeezed his fingers. She couldn't remember a time she was more content.

Rip shot a twisted smile at her. "How would you rank this as a first date?"

"Right up there." She sipped her cocoa. "Although I don't think most first dates last an entire week."

"No?" Rip stood and took the mug from her hands. "Well, we have your boss to thank for that. It was nice of him to offer his mountain cabin for your recuperation and the plane to get us here in comfort." Rip eased her out of her chair and into his arms, so careful not to disturb her stitches.

Tracie leaned into him, wrapping her arms around his rock-hard waist and resting her cheek against his chiseled chest. Feeling very lucky to have him, she lifted her face and stood on her toes to press a kiss to Rip's lips. He tasted of marshmallows and cocoa and she loved it. "Mmm. Remind me to thank Hank."

Despite the tug at her stitches, she didn't want the kiss to end and pushed up on her toes again, deepening it until their tongues writhed together and her body heated.

The cell phone on the table beside the lounge chair buzzed and vibrated, shattering the silence of the mountainside.

Rip looked up, brushing a strand of her hair behind her ear. "Should we answer it?"

Tracie shook her head. "No."

Rip glanced at the cell phone. "It's yours and, if I'm not mistaken, it's Hank."

Tracie sighed and bent to grab the phone. "Kosart here."

"Tracie, are you with Rip?"

She smiled, tipping her head so that the man in question could nibble her neck. "Yes, sir, I am."

"Turn on the television."

Tracie couldn't think straight with Rip's lips angling lower, his hands parting her silk robe. "What?"

"Put me on speaker," Hank demanded.

She hit the button for speakerphone and Hank's voice came over loud and clear, "Turn on the television. Senator Craine is about to make a statement on live TV."

Rip sighed. "Come on." He slipped an arm around her waist, guided her back into the cabin and hit the on button for the state-of-the-art video system. It had taken him half an hour to figure out all the controls, but he had them down now.

Following Hank's instructions, they found the channel and waited.

Senator Craine appeared in front of a podium with several microphones. He started by stating that he didn't have any idea that his executive assistant Mark Kuntz was running arms to rebel fighters in Honduras and that he was sorry for the deaths of the DEA agent and the SEAL who'd been sent in to retrieve him. While he made his statement, a disturbance occurred as uniformed FBI agents pushed through the crowd, walked up onto the stage and cuffed the senator.

The reporter covering the story described what was happening in an excited tone. "They're charging him with treason and misappropriation of government equipment!"

The press went wild, cameras flashed and the senator was led away.

Shocked, Tracie stood with her mouth open, struggling to comprehend what had just occurred.

"Tracie? Rip?" Hank's voice sounded nearby and Tracie realized she hadn't hung up.

"What the hell just happened?" she asked.

Hank laughed. "Brandon kept digging and found the bank accounts that connected Craine to Kuntz's dirty dealings with Delgado and the terrorist training camp. It just took longer than we expected. Although, I can't argue with the timing. Perhaps the public arrest of Senator Craine will serve as a reminder to our other elected officials to keep it clean."

"We can always hope." Tracie shook her head. "You don't know who to trust anymore."

"You can trust me," Hank said.

"And me." Rip kissed her cheek and leaned over the phone she still held. "Hank, just in case I didn't tell you before, thanks for this week, and for sending Tracie to help me. You couldn't have picked a better cowboy from Covert Cowboys, Inc."

"Glad to be of service," Hank said. "And thank you for your service. The Citation will be there tomorrow to take you back to Mississippi where your unit is anxious to receive you with a hero's welcome."

"I don't know about hero." Rip's hand slid around Tracie's waist and he dropped a kiss on her forehead. "Gosling was the hero."

"Speaking of Gosling," Hank said. "I've set up a trust fund for his wife and baby. They won't want for anything for the rest of their lives."

A lump formed in Tracie's throat. She knew money couldn't replace a husband and father.

She glanced up at Rip, noting the sheen of moisture in his eyes. He'd been thinking the same thing.

"Thanks, Hank," Rip said.

Tracie hung up and leaned into Rip's embrace. "I feel so bad for Gosling's widow and child."

"I know Jeanette." Rip smoothed Tracie's hair back and tipped her head up so that he could stare into her eyes. "I even asked her if she'd have done anything different if she had known he'd die. She said no. She loved him with all her heart and knew the risks that came with loving a SEAL."

"She would have wanted every moment of happiness she could grab," Tracie finished, finally understanding that concept.

"So CCI Agent Kosart," Rip pressed a featherlight kiss to the tip of her nose. "What's it to be? Are you ready to end what we just started?"

She leaned up on her toes and pressed a kiss to his lips. "No way in hell." She wrapped her arms around him and held on tight. "I'm going for all the happiness I can squeeze into the time we have together."

"Are you going to come visit me in Mississippi or anywhere else I might be stationed?"

"Wild horses couldn't keep me away." She stared up at him. "Would you mind terribly if I stayed with you between my CCI assignments?"

Rip's lips spread into a wide grin and he laughed out loud. "Honey, I wouldn't have it any other way."

\* \* \* \* \*

## #1575 SURRENDERING TO THE SHERIFF
*Sweetwater Ranch* • by Delores Fossen
Discovering Kendall O'Neal being held at gunpoint at his ranch isn't the homecoming sheriff Aiden Braddock expects. Kendall's captors are demanding he destroy evidence in exchange for the Texas attorney's life... and the life of their unborn baby.

## #1576 UNDER FIRE
*Brothers in Arms: Retribution* • by Carol Ericson
Agent Max Duvall needs Dr. Ava Whitman's help to break free from the brainwashing that Tempest—the covert ops agency they work for—has subjected him to...but he's going to have to keep the agency from killing her first.

## #1577 SHELTERED
*Corcoran Team: Bulletproof Bachelors* • by HelenKay Dimon
Undercover agent Holt Kingston has one mission: to infiltrate a dangerous cult. But when the compound's ruthless leader has a gorgeous former member in his sights, single-minded Holt won't rest until Lindsey Pike is safe.

## #1578 LAWMAN PROTECTION
*The Ranger Brigade* • by Cindi Myers
A killer is lurking in Colorado, and reporter Emma Wade is sniffing around Captain Graham Ellison's crime scene. As much as he doesn't want a civilian accessing his case, Graham will need to keep Emma close if he is going to keep her alive.

## #1579 LEVERAGE
*Omega Sector* • by Janie Crouch
Reclusive pilot Dylan Branson's mission to escort Shelby Keelan to Omega Sector goes awry after his plane is sabotaged midair. With both their lives in danger, Dylan no longer thinks Shelby is just a job—or that he can let her go once it's over.

## #1580 THE DETECTIVE • by Adrienne Giordano
Passion ignites when interior designer Lexi Vanderbilt teams up with hardened homicide detective Brodey Hayward to solve a cold case murder. But will Lexi's ambition make them both targets of a killer?

---

**YOU CAN FIND MORE INFORMATION ON UPCOMING HARLEQUIN® TITLES, FREE EXCERPTS AND MORE AT WWW.HARLEQUIN.COM.**

HICNM0615

"How do I know you really work for Hank?"

"You don't. But has anyone else shown up and told you he's your contact?" She raised her eyebrows, the saucy expression doing funny things to his insides. "So, do you trust me, or not?"

His lips curled upward on the ends. "I'll go with not."

"Oh, come on, sweetheart." She batted her pretty green eyes and gave him a sexy smile. "What's not to trust?"

His gaze scraped over her form. "I expected a cowboy, not a…"

"Cow*girl*?" Her smile sank and she slipped into the driver's seat. Her lips firmed into a straight line. "Are you coming or not? If you're dead set on a cowboy, I'll contact Hank and tell him to send a male replacement. But then he'd have to come up with another plan."

"I'm interested in how you and Hank plan to help. Frankly, I'd rather my SEAL team had my six."

"Yeah, but you're deceased. Using your SEAL team would only alert your assassin that you aren't as dead as the navy claims you are. How long do you think you'll last once that bit of news leaks out?"

His lips pressed together. "I'd survive."

"By going undercover? Then you still won't have the backing of your team, and we're back to the original plan." She grinned. "Me."

Rip sighed. "Fine. I want to head back to Honduras and trace the weapons back to where they're coming from. What's Hank's plan?"

"For me to work with you." She pulled a large envelope from between her seat and the console and handed it across to him. "Everything we need is in that packet."

Rip riffled through the contents of the packet, glancing at a passport with his picture on it as well as a name he'd never seen. "Chuck Gideon?"

"Better get used to it."

"Speaking of names...we've already kissed and you haven't told me who you are." Rip glanced her way briefly. "Is it a secret? Do you have a shady past or are you related to someone important?"

"For this mission, I'm related to someone important." She twisted her lips and sent a crooked grin his way. "You. For the purpose of this operation, you can call me Phyllis. Phyllis Gideon. I'll be your wife."

*Don't miss*
*NAVY SEAL NEWLYWED,*
*available June 2015 wherever*
*Harlequin® Intrigue® books and ebooks are sold*

www.Harlequin.com

# Praise for *Wanna Get Lucky?*

"*Wanna Get Lucky?* sizzles. It beguiles and surprises. It's belly-laugh funny. Add in unforgettable characters, crimes to die for, the *ka-ching* of high-stakes casinos, and Laura Ashley–decorated bordellos, and you have a read that's utterly irresistible from first page to last. Watch out, Janet Evanovich. The new hot number is Deborah Coonts!"

> —Gayle Lynds, *New York Times*
> bestselling author of *The Book of Spies*

"*Wanna Get Lucky?* is a winner on every level. Deborah Coonts has crafted a first-class murder mystery coupled with a touching and unexpected love story. Against a flawlessly rendered Las Vegas backdrop, Lucky's story is funny, fast paced, exuberant, and brilliantly realized."

> —Susan Wiggs, *New York Times*
> bestselling author of *Just Breathe*

"Lucky O'Toole is a character with brains, beauty, and a wry sense of humor. Readers will want to meet her again—and soon."

> —Diane Mott Davidson, *New York Times*
> bestselling author of *Fatally Flaky*

"*Wanna Get Lucky?* is an amazing debut novel, a mile-a-minute read, fantastic characters, dry wit, and the gritty neon feel of Las Vegas. Bravo to Deborah Coonts—I see a great future ahead!"

> —Heather Graham, *New York Times*
> bestselling author of *Night of the Wolves*